"Why do you affect me so strongly?"

Seth's voice was quiet as he continued. "There's something about you, Tascha...I can't seem to help myself. I've never wanted to touch a woman the way I want to touch you." Lowering his hand to caress her cheek, he added, but almost in anger, "Why do you do this to me? What is it about you? You've lied to me and deceived me—I don't even *like* you!"

Desperate to protect herself and angered at her vulnerability to Seth's final words, Tascha lashed out coldly, "I presume that the message is you want me physically, Seth, but you're not interested in me as a person."

"So that's how you see it," Seth drew back sharply, visibly retreating from her. "Perhaps you're right," he added, but with an indifference that seemed strangely forced.

SANDRA FIELD, once a biology technician, now writes full-time. She lives with her son in Canada's Maritimes, which she often uses as a setting for her books. She loves the independent life-style she has as a writer. She's her own boss, sets her own hours, and increasingly there are travel opportunities.

Books by Sandra Field

HARLEQUIN PRESENTS

HARLEQUIN ROMANCE

writing as Jan MacLean

writing as Jocelyn Haley

DREAM OF DARKNESS

HARLEQUIN SUPERROMANCE

Don't miss any of our special offers. Write to us at the following address for information on our newest releases.

Harlequin Reader Service
901 Fuhrmann Blvd., P.O. Box 1397, Buffalo, NY 14240
Canadian address: P.O. Box 603,
Fort Erie, Ont. L2A 5X3

SANDRA FIELD

chase a rainbow

Harlequin Books

TORONTO • NEW YORK • LONDON
AMSTERDAM • PARIS • SYDNEY • HAMBURG
STOCKHOLM • ATHENS • TOKYO • MILAN

Harlequin Presents first edition April 1989
ISBN 0-373-11159-2

Original hardcover edition published in 1988
by Mills & Boon Limited

CHAPTER ONE

ALL day as the plane had flown west from Montreal Tascha had focused on Whitehorse as her destination: Whitehorse, capital of the Yukon, three thousand miles west of Montreal, a thousand miles north of Vancouver. But now she had arrived in Whitehorse, and as she entered the terminal, which was large and impersonal, she realised with a tightening of her nerves that her journey had only just begun.

She had learned, in this her first day of air travel, to follow the crowd. Dependably, her fellow passengers now led her to the baggage carousel. She waited impatiently until her canvas bag appeared, then headed for the airline ticket counter across an expanse of pale, gleaming floor. But at the last minute her steps faltered and her throat went dry. What if they had never heard of the lodge? What if it had closed down years ago? She had been a fool to fly out here without making enquiries first. As was so often the case, her behaviour had been impulsive and irrational. She could hear Olga's strident voice ring in her ears, criticising her for just those traits, and shivered inwardly, for Olga was not long dead and certainly not forgotten.

'May I help you, madam?'

The ticket agent was a pretty brunette with a friendly smile. 'I hope so,' Tascha said, her English, as always, carrying the slight intonation of one who speaks another language just as familiarly. 'I want to go to Caribou Lodge. It's run by Neil Curtis. Do you have any idea of how I get there?'

The brunette frowned in thought. 'One of the charter companies goes that way, I believe. But I'm not sure which one.'

Some of the tension in Tascha's shoulders loosened; so the lodge *did* exist. Perhaps she had not been a fool, after all.

The ticket agent glanced the length of the counter. 'If Chuck was here he could tell you. But he's off duty until tomorrow morning. Tell you what—see the little shop over there? Check with Lily, the woman at the cash register. Lily knows everything there is to know about the charter planes; one of her sons flew for them for years.'

In Montreal, Tascha's home town, one would not be sent to the gift shop to find out about charter flights. More of her tension dissolving in amusement, Tascha smiled at the brunette, said, 'Thank you,' and walked across to the shop, her bag banging against her knee.

She was wearing jeans, a loose blue T-shirt and sneakers, all of them well worn, none of them distinguished in price or design; and her bag was the cheapest kind of carry-all. But as Tascha crossed the high-ceilinged room to the shop she attracted several second glances. Although her hair was ash-blonde, gathered into a fat braid down her back, and although her eyes were a clear, true blue, it was less these attributes that drew attention than her elegant cheekbones, her high-arched forehead and her exquisitely sculpted lips. She would not have been out of place on the cover of *Vogue* or *Elle*, swathed in mink and ablaze with sapphires; and she wore the cheap clothing with an unconscious air of distinction, as if they were indeed mink and sapphires.

Lily was ringing up a sale when Tascha entered the shop. Lily had red hair, red lipstick, and a red sweater stretched tightly over an ample bust; consequently she looked less like a lily than an overblown rose. She finished discussing the weather, which apparently had been unusually wet, with the man ahead of Tascha and switched her smile over to Tascha. It was a smile every bit as genuine as the brunette's. 'C'n I help you, dear?'

Swallowing the tightness that had seized her throat again, Tascha gulped, 'I hope so. I'm trying to find out which of the charter companies flies to the lodge that Neil Curtis runs. Caribou Lodge. I want to go there.'

'Well, now, dear, Neil isn't running the lodge any more.' A tremendous sigh wobbled the red-covered bosom. 'Neil isn't running anything any more—they buried him four months ago.'

A response was obviously expected. 'Oh,' said Tascha weakly, 'I'm sorry. I never knew him—was he an old man?'

This was not the question she wanted to ask. She wanted to cry out, is the lodge still operating? Can I get there tomorrow? However, Lily was almost certainly not one to be hurried. Even now she was resting her elbows on the cash register and leaning forward confidentially.

'Not a day over sixty, dear, and a fine-looking man.' Lily sighed lugubriously. 'I might as well tell you that since my Dan passed on I kind of looked in Neil's direction myself. Yeah, I sure did. Might as well have saved myself the trouble, though. Neil never had eyes for anyone after his wife died, and that's twenty years ago, easy. Never even looked at another woman, and him with a son growing up half-wild. Ah, well, that's the way of the world.' And she paused politely to allow Tascha time to commiserate.

'So is the lodge closed down?' Tascha blurted.

'Oh, no, dear, Seth wouldn't do that. Seth's been running it for years, anyway, after his father kind of lost interest in it along with everything else. A heart attack, that's what took Neil. Had a broken heart for years, if you ask me. And him such a fine figure of a man.' Another huge sigh shook Lily's frame.

While Lily was undoubtedly overpowering, she was also possessed of kindness and a zest for life; deciding that Neil Curtis sounded a bit spineless, no matter what a fine figure he had had, Tascha said bluntly, 'So how do I get to the lodge?'

'Mackenzie Air. Their hangar is two over from the terminal.' Shrewdly, Lily sized up Tascha's outfit. 'It'll cost you a pretty penny, dear.'

For once in her life, money was the least of Tascha's worries. 'I seem to have spent quite a lot already,' she said, rather to her own surprise, for she was not one to volunteer information about herself. 'I'll phone them tomorrow morning and see if I can get a reservation.'

'You might even be able to go back with Seth...oh, excuse me, dear.' Lily sold two boxes of cigars to a man whose florid complexion indicated he would be better off without them, and turned back to Tascha. 'Seth's in town right now. Why don't you speak to him first?'

The glimpse Tascha had had of Whitehorse when the plane had broken through low-lying clouds had shown her a city of some size on either side of the winding, blue-green Yukon River. 'Where would I find him?'

'White's Hotel. He always stays there. It would be best if you could go to the lodge with him, dear—the plane doesn't exactly land on the doorstep, you know.' Lily laughed loudly at her own joke.

Not sure what Lily meant by this, Tascha asked, 'How would I know him?'

'Seth?' Lily rolled her eyes. 'Why, he's just the best-looking man in the Yukon, that's all.'

Tascha found herself smiling. 'Like father, like son?' she teased.

Lily pursed her lips. 'Well, I do have to admit that Seth's got more get up and go than his daddy ever had.

Takes after his mother, does Seth. Got her black hair and black eyes. But the rest of him's all man, believe you me. Tall—I do like a tall man, don't you, dear?—and shoulders on him like...like Rambo,' Lily finished triumphantly.

Tascha had assiduously avoided the Rambo movies. She said diplomatically, 'I'm sure I'll find him if I ask for him at the hotel. Maybe I'll stay there tonight myself.'

'It's an OK place. You won't run into any trouble there.'

Tascha picked up a chocolate bar and a couple of magazines, paid for them and said sincerely, 'Thank you, Lily, for all your help.'

'Pleasure, dear. Hope you find Seth. You'd look cute with him, being so small and blonde and him so big and dark...makes me wish I was your age all over again.' Lily raised her eyebrows expressively and waved a cheery goodbye.

As Tascha lifted a hand in salute, she decided that if Lily had been alive ninety years ago, in the gold rush, she would have been running a saloon. It would unquestionably have been the most successful saloon in town!

She headed for the exit, where she took a taxi to White's Hotel. Her eyes scarcely registered the rain-soaked landscape. The lodge still existed, she thought. She would find this Seth Curtis and he would take her there, and the first part of her mission would be accomplished. Beyond that, at the moment, she could not go. The man she sought remained a shadowy, mysterious figure, as remote from her in this northern city as he had been in the cramped little apartment in Montreal when she had first read about him in the letters hidden in Olga's drawer.

White's Hotel had no pretensions to architectural grandeur, being a cream stucco box on a street corner downtown. But the paint was fresh and the hall was clean, although crowded with artificial rubber trees and carpeted in a black and orange shag-pile. Tascha paid for her room and accepted the key, deciding she would enquire about Seth Curtis later; she did not have the energy right now to face anyone who looked like Rambo.

The room was also very clean, and the water in the bathroom steamingly hot. Tascha soaked in the tub, feeling the tiredness of a long day of jet travel gradually leave her. Then she put on a pair of beige trousers with a pink shirt, arranged her hair in a loose ponytail and went down to the hotel dining-room for dinner. The food was plentiful and hot. She read her magazine, paid for the meal, and went to the front desk. The proprietress was larger than Lily, without any of Lily's buoyancy, and said to Tascha without enthusiasm, 'I hope your room is to your satisfaction?'

'It's fine, thanks...I'm trying to locate someone who's also a guest in the hotel—Seth Curtis. You wouldn't know if he's in his room, would you?'

The smallest sign of interest showed in the woman's heavy features. 'Seth? He went out for dinner. To the Pioneer Room, that's two blocks south. You might catch him there.'

'If not, then perhaps I can leave a message with you when I get back?'

'You could do that. He's not usually back until late.' While Lily would probably walk five miles to deliver a message to Seth, Tascha doubted this woman would walk the length of her desk. Deciding, not for the first time, that it was the infinite variety in human beings that made life interesting, she smiled politely and went to get her rain-jacket.

Because Whitehorse was so far north, the streets were not yet dark. The Pioneer Room, swathed in gloomy mock-oak panelling and dimly lit, seemed darker than

the outdoors, certainly too dark for Tascha to pick out
the best-looking man in the Yukon from among the
diners. She said to the hostess, 'Could you tell me if
Seth Curtis is here, please?' and wondered if she had
been wise in tracing the man to a place so obviously
designed for ultra-discreet tête-à-têtes; he would not be
in the best of moods if she interrupted a romantic
rendezvous. But she had to find him, because he might
leave for the lodge early the next morning.

'He just left. Got a phone call from the Scagway and
took off in a hurry. Be a good place to steer clear of for
the next half-hour,' said the hostess, who had dyed hair,
a frilly uniform and tired eyes.

'What's the Scagway?' Tascha said blankly.

'You a visitor? Roughest tavern in town, that's what
the Scagway is. And if Seth's headed over there you can
bet your bottom dollar it won't be getting any quieter.'

Tascha had a sudden vision of Sylvester Stallone, with
a red band around his forehead, spraying the Scagway
Tavern with machine-gun bullets; the more she heard
about Seth Curtis, the less he sounded like someone she
would care to travel with. 'Well, I'd better see if I can
find him.'

The hostess rested her hand on Tascha's sleeve. 'Don't
you go in there, now. The Scagway's no place for a
tourist, let alone one as pretty as you.'

The woman was genuinely alarmed. Tascha said,
without actually lying, 'I won't do anything silly, I
promise. Thanks for your help,' and left. Outside, she
asked the first pedestrian she met, a grey-haired man in
a stetson, for directions to the Scagway Tavern.

'Two blocks to the right, one down. No place for a
woman,' he said economically, and kept on walking.

The façade of the Scagway was not prepossessing, with
its dark-stained wood, two dirty windows coated with
black paper so no one could see inside, and much-kicked

doors that swung on hinges and could have been props in a Clint Eastwood movie. Although Tascha was not Clint Eastwood, she had grown up in one of the poorest sections of Montreal and she very much wanted to meet Seth Curtis. She buttoned her jacket to her chin and pushed open the door.

Two short, angled corridors led to the main area of the tavern. Tascha took the right-hand one, and stationed herself in the doorway where she could survey the whole room. No one paid her the slightest bit of attention. The silence was absolute.

In the middle of the smoke-wreathed room, a black-haired man with burning black eyes was holding another man off the floor by the simple expedient of two fists clenched in the man's checked shirt; incongruously, the black-haired man was wearing a white dress-shirt and a tie. The eyes of everyone in the room were on this little tableau, save those of a youth slumped over one of the centre tables, his head buried in his arms. For a horrible moment, during which she wished she had heeded all the warnings about the iniquitous Scagway, Tascha thought he was dead. But then he stirred a little, the fringes of his calfskin jacket swaying back and forth, before growing still again.

Into the silence, the black-haired man said in a deep voice that reverberated with rage, 'You brought him in here, didn't you, Slim?'

Slim was the man in the checked shirt, who weighed at least two hundred pounds and whose face was so red he looked as if he might explode. He choked out an expletive that Tascha, probably luckily, could not decipher. It did not noticeably impress the black-haired man, who was, even under the stress of the present moment, extremely good-looking. Tascha was ninety-nine per cent sure that she had found Seth Curtis;

however, it did not seem to be the time to walk up to him and ask him for a ride to Caribou Lodge.

'Answer the question, Slim,' Seth Curtis grated, lifting Slim a little higher from the ground.

'Yeah, I brought him here! Don't know why you're making such a fuss—he's only a dumb kid who's had a couple of beers too many.'

'He's a friend of mine, Slim,' Seth Curtis said very softly. 'He's on probation and he's not supposed to be anywhere near this place. You know that as well as I do. The reason you know is because I told you last week— right?'

'I forgot,' Slim mumbled. 'C'mon, Seth, you know how it is—I'd had a few beers myself and I forgot what you told me.'

With a dramatic suddenness, Seth dropped Slim to the floor. The audience, which was exclusively male, let out an appreciative communal sigh. Tascha had never seen such concentrated ferocity in a man's face as when Seth said with the same dangerous quietness, 'Do you plan on forgetting again, Slim? Because, if you do, I'll give you something right now to make you remember.'

'I won't forget again, Seth, swear to God I won't!'

'Let's leave God out of it. If I hear you so much as breathe the word beer within fifty feet of that kid, I'll have your hide for a saddlebag.'

Slim gave an unconvincing laugh. 'Sure, Seth, sure...you know I won't forget again.'

'Don't—that's my advice.'

Very deliberately, Seth Curtis turned his back on the red-faced man in the checked shirt and walked over to the table where the youth was slumped. In a single lithe movement he hauled the lad over his shoulder and began walking towards the door where Tascha was standing. He had very broad shoulders, she had time to think, and was strong enough to flip her out of his way without as much as batting an eyelid. Or, judging by the scowl on his face, to walk right through her without even noticing her!

The men in the room had swivelled in their seats to watch Seth's progress, and were now watching her with a deep appreciation for drama. The part of her that Olga had never entirely been able to quell rose to the occasion. She drew herself up to her full five feet six inches and said in her clearest voice, 'Excuse me, please . . . are you Seth Curtis?'

The black-haired man stopped two feet away from her. He was not quite as omnipotent as he had looked, because there were beads of sweat on his forehead and lines of strain around his mouth; but he was quite definitely the most handsome man she had ever seen, in the Yukon or out of it. He said flatly, 'Yes. I don't know who you are, but this is the last place a woman should be.'

Discovering she was tired of that line, Tascha said, 'I've already been told that by two other people.'

'Then perhaps you should listen.'

'I came here because I wanted to talk to you.'

'But I'm about to leave. As you see.'

Tascha held her ground. 'Then can we talk outside?'

'Certainly there would be fewer eavesdroppers.' Even with the youth draped over his shoulder, Seth Curtis managed a mocking bow. 'After you, madam.'

A titter ran round the room. 'You gonna stand there half the night staring at a pretty girl, Seth?' one of the drinkers yelled.

'Lots of pretty girls around here, Seth—you know that.'

'What d'you figure she wants?' someone called from the back of the room, and a bass voice to the left furnished a decidedly obscene reply.

Tascha's eyes glittered furiously. Forgetting about Seth, she pivoted on her heel and told the bass voice in street French exactly where it could go. Then she stalked out of the Scagway Tavern.

Said the deep voice behind her, 'My dear young woman, wherever did you learn such deplorable language?'

She turned to face him on the pavement, where the overhead light made an angelic halo of her hair, and said pithily, 'Since you understood me, I could ask you the same question.'

The amusement in his face was heightened by another emotion, one altogether more intense, but all he said was, 'Montreal.'

'I, also.'

He said abruptly, 'You wanted to talk to me—can't it wait until tomorrow?'

'I've come a long way,' she said, afraid that if he left her now she might never see him again.

His black eyes seemed to bore right through her. He said, not very graciously, 'I have to take Jonah home. If you came with me we could talk on the way back— he lives three or four miles out of town.' With a sideways jerk of his head, he indicated a red jeep parked by the kerb.

In a strange city, thousands of miles from home, Tascha should not have got into a vehicle with two unknown men, one of whom was very drunk, the other of whom could pick her up with one hand. But all the rules had been broken when she had found the letters in Olga's drawer. She said, 'Thank you. I'd appreciate that.'

Seth Curtis strapped his burden into the front seat. The boy muttered something under his breath, then lolled against the closed door. Tascha climbed in the back. It was still raining.

Seth drove in silence, soon leaving the lights of the city behind. They turned up a dirt road, unlit, the forest crowding to the ditches. Stones rattled under the wheels.

The wipers swished back and forth. In the reflected light from the dashboard Tascha could see Seth Curtis's profile: strongly hewn, immobile, its strength matched by its innate intelligence, an intelligence she was quite sure Rambo could not match. She recognised that deep within her she was a little afraid of him, and would have been more afraid had Lily not vouched for him. Seth had had a father who had allowed him to grow up half-wild and who had died of a broken heart, and a mother with black hair and black eyes; he could pick up a two-hundred-pound man and keep a roomful of drunks mesmerised; he understood the kind of French that was not taught in universities. And, she added reluctantly, his hair curled on the nape of his neck in a way that made her long to touch it. She was not in the habit of touching strangers.

Firmly she sat on her hands. She would find out more about him before she set off to Caribou Lodge; and she would be sure to tell him only what she wanted him to know.

The jeep careened along the road, which seemed to be in desperate need of grading. She had not realised the depth of her uneasiness until she saw through the close-spaced trees a flicker of lights. A house. People. Something to break the blackness of the night.

Seth slowed, then pulled up in front of a small wooden bungalow, its walls coated with tar paper, its windows curtainless. A dog began to bark. He turned off the engine, said, 'I might be a while,' and got out of the jeep. Rounding its hood, he slid the young man over his shoulder again and carried him across an expanse of churned-up mud to the front steps of the bungalow. The door opened before he could knock. He disappeared inside.

Tascha sat very still. The rain pattered on the roof of the jeep. The dog was howling now, long, falsetto howls of such loneliness that she wanted to hold her hands to her ears to shut them out. The darkness seemed to press against the windows of the jeep, much as the black paper had been pressed against the windows of the Scagway Tavern. All the bravado with which she had faced Seth Curtis had vanished. She felt frightened and very much alone. No one in the world—apart from Seth—knew where she was right now. No one cared.

But worse than the loneliness was the disorientation from which she had been suffering ever since she had read the two letters in Olga's drawer just the day before yesterday. She was twenty-two years old and, since she had been old enough to consider such things, had thought she knew who she was: Tascha Dennis, daughter of Olga Dennis, resident of the Pointe Saint-Charles district of Montreal. Poor. Pretty. Too clever for her own good.

She had never known a father, never even known his name, for Olga had refused to discuss him, retreating into a tight-lipped silence if the subject ever came up, and an icy, terrifying rage on the few occasions when Tascha had persisted in her questions. Tascha had tried hard to love her mother and win her approval, and one of the bitterest lessons of her teenage years had been the recognition that both goals were impossible, for Olga loved no one and disapproved of everyone—most of all her wayward, blue-eyed daughter.

Olga had died very suddenly of a heart attack two weeks ago. Since her death, Tascha had discovered a bank account in Olga's name which contained the astonishing sum of ten thousand dollars, money whose source was a total mystery to her. And when, reluctantly, she had gone through Olga's few personal effects in the tiny front bedroom of their apartment, she had found at the very back of a drawer, under a pile of cheap flannelette nightgowns, two letters. The postmarks were twenty years old. The handwriting, fine and elegant, was un-known to her. The letters were addressed to Olga Denisov, care of general delivery. Each was signed, simply, 'Belov'.

After a brief moral struggle, because the letters were not addressed to her, Tascha had read them. The gist of the first letter was that the writer had fortuitously made a new friend in Whitehorse, Neil Curtis by name, owner of an establishment called Caribou Lodge in the Northwest Territories, and that very soon a place would be in order where Olga and the child could join him. The second letter had burned itself into Tascha's brain on the very first reading.

> 'My dear Olga,
>
> I am sorry I have not written sooner. But your news devastated me, for in the death of the child I have lost the last living memory of my beloved Marya. What else can I say? You had no need to assure me you did everything you could—I know that and I thank you from the bottom of my heart for your care of the child. I am enclosing all my savings as a gift for you, Olga. I hope the money will enable you to establish yourself in a new life in this vast country.
>
> Be assured of my continued affection,
>
> Belov.'

Tascha had read and reread the two letters, searching for every nuance of meaning, her brain buzzing with questions. Denisov and Belov were surely Russian names, as were Olga, Tascha and Marya. Who was the man called Belov who had found a home in the remote northern wilderness and who had wanted Olga and 'the child' to join him? Who was 'the child?' Could it possibly have been herself? Could Olga have lied about

the child's death to the man called Belov, and then raised
the child as her own child, as Tascha Dennis? But why?
Why? And that was the question Tascha could not possibly answer, for Olga was dead and the secrets of the
past, if indeed there were any, had died with her.

But the possibility, slight though it was, that she,
Tascha, might not be Olga's child, had been enough to
make her heart beat fast with a desperate longing. She
had tried so hard to love Olga and to be loved in return,
and had failed, and the guilt for that failure had been
with her for as long as she could remember. But, if Olga
was not her true mother, if 'my beloved Marya' was her
mother, then she could forgive herself for that failure.
For Olga must have hated the man called Belov to have
lied to him about his child's death, and that hatred would
have transferred itself to Tascha.

But every time she came to this point in her reflections
Tascha would throw up her hands in despair. She was
making castles in the air, constructing dream worlds because she did not like the world of reality. Olga was her
mother. Olga had to be her mother. She had lived with
Olga for as long as she could remember, and had been
told she had been born in the old hospital near Mont
Royal... On the other hand, she had lived in poverty
for as long as she could remember, and yet Olga had
died with ten thousand dollars in a private account.
Could that be the money mentioned in the letter?

Around and around her thoughts had whirled, chasing
each other in ever smaller circles, until she had suddenly
roused herself, gone to the bank and arranged a loan on
the basis of the money in the account, made bookings
for Whitehorse at the travel agency and packed her bag.
She would go to Whitehorse and find the man called
Belov and ask if the name of the child had been Tascha.

And now she was waiting in a jeep owned by Neil
Curtis's son, who ran Caribou Lodge. Seth Curtis might

know the man called Belov. Might take her to him tomorrow. Because the thought was enough to make her palms damp with sweat, she forced herself to listen to the cold voice of reason. Belov could be dead, just as Neil Curtis was dead. Belov could have moved a thousand miles away twenty years ago, when he discovered he no longer had to furnish a home for his daughter. He could have disappeared without a trace into the vastness that was Canada. Which meant she would never know who she was.

Tascha pressed her hands against her face, beating down a suffocating wave of despair. She must not think in such a way. She must not allow herself to be defeated so easily. Seth Curtis would take her to Belov. She had to hold tightly to that thought.

CHAPTER TWO

SLOWLY Tascha lowered her hands. The rain trickled down the windscreen of the jeep like tears down a cheek. The bungalow remained closed against her. She shivered a little, for the air was damp and cold, and felt a twinge of anger towards Seth Curtis, who had turned off the engine and abandoned her to the weather. She glanced through the window again. The door of the bungalow was tightly shut.

Seth had left the keys in the ignition. Trusting of him, she thought ironically. Had it not occurred to him that a young woman who had braved the Scagway Tavern might be tempted to drive off with his jeep? She wriggled from the back seat into the driver's seat, avoiding the clutch, and after studying the controls for a few moments put on the emergency brake, shifted to neutral and turned on the engine. Then she pushed the heater levers to 'HOT' and 'FLOOR'.

Two things happened. A blast of warm air eddied about her ankles, and the front door of the bungalow burst open. Seth Curtis took the narrow wooden steps two at a time and crossed the yard in few strides. He flung open the door of the jeep. 'Where the hell d'you think you're going?' he demanded.

His face was so close that she could admire the length and thickness of his lashes, and again she felt that absurd, fleeting longing to touch him, she who rarely touched anyone. 'Nowhere,' she snapped. 'I was cold.'

'Cold? You think this is cold?' He gave a short laugh. 'You should be here in February.'

21

'You've been inside a heated bungalow. I've been waiting—for some time, I might add—in a very draughty jeep.'

Instead of looking sorry, Seth began to smile. His teeth were very white. 'I said I'd be a while. And, if I recall correctly, I didn't invite you here—you invited yourself.'

She could feel herself being drawn into the blackness of his eyes, in which laughter lurked almost irresistibly. She said stiffly, 'You're getting wet, you'd better get in,' and moved over into the passenger's seat.

Seth climbed in, gave a blast of the horn and a wave of his hand to the two men standing silhouetted in the front window of the bungalow, and reversed back on the road. Tascha, who had planned to ask him immediately about Caribou Lodge and the man called Belov, heard herself say, 'Will your friend Jonah be all right?'

'He'll have a hangover tomorrow. No more than he deserves.'

'Why were you so angry with Slim?'

'That's between Slim and me, surely.'

'Plus all the occupants of the Scagway.'

'But nothing to do with you!'

Stung, Tascha snapped, 'I was just interested, that's all. What's the matter—are you afraid of showing that you're human?'

Seth's hands tightened on the wheel. Looking straight ahead of him, he said emotionlessly, 'Jonah's been in trouble with the law before, so he's on probation. He's a half-breed Indian, so he doesn't get many of the financial benefits that a full-blooded Indian gets; but I've been trying to encourage him to go to university, take some control over his life. If the police had caught him in the Scagway tonight, he'd have landed in jail— which is hardly taking control of your life. Slim knows Jonah's got a drinking problem and he knows about the probation, too—but he took him in the Scagway, anyway.

Like everyone else around here, he thinks it's a big joke that I bother with a half-breed kid who can't handle his liquor.'

She remembered that Seth had left his dinner in the Pioneer Room to find Jonah, and she remembered his repressed rage towards Slim. 'I don't think it's a joke. At least you care enough to try.'

'I suppose ... I might take him to Vancouver with me in the fall, get him away from all his drinking buddies.'

He had given her an opening. 'Don't you live at the lodge all year round?'

'The season's two months at the most,' Seth said drily. 'The rest of the year you'd be snowed in.'

Very much aware of her ignorance, Tascha said humbly, 'Lily gave me your name at the airport. She said you'd be going back to the lodge very soon. I wondered if I could go with you.'

He took his eyes from the road to glance sideways at her. 'Sorry,' he said. 'We're booked up.'

She gaped at him in dismay, for if she had anticipated a refusal it had been on the basis that he might not want to travel with her. 'Booked *up*?' she squeaked. 'How can you be?'

There was the same dry note in his voice. 'Quite easily. The lodge has a maximum capacity of twelve guests. There are twelve guests there right now, and twelve different ones arriving at the end of the week.'

'You can't be full for the rest of the summer!'

'Not only that, but I've started getting reservations already for next year. Caribou Lodge has been running for years, so it's very well known among a certain group of people who want what we offer.'

'But I really want to go there!'

'Then make a reservation now for next year. Barring fire, flood, or pestilence, we'll still be around.'

'I want to go now!' Tascha said frantically. 'Please, Mr Curtis, couldn't you make an exception? I'll sleep on the floor if I have to, and I promise I won't make a nuisance of myself. *Please!*'

She was stretching out her hands in unconscious pleading. He said curiously, 'Why is it so important to you?' and must have seen her face change as she drew back into herself.

'I—my reasons are personal,' she mumbled.

'Where are you from?'

'Montreal.'

'You've just arrived?'

'Today.'

'You came all the way out here to go to the lodge without checking first to see if we had any openings?'

His voice could have been Olga's, exalting the virtues of common sense over impulse. Tascha stared sullenly at the hands in her lap.

'I don't even know your name,' Seth Curtis said.

'Tascha Dennis.'

'Who told you about the lodge?'

She was silent, for the letters in Olga's drawer were too private to share with a stranger.

He said impatiently, 'Quite apart from anything else, have you any idea of how much a week at the lodge will cost you?'

They were driving down the hill towards the city. In sudden panic, Tascha realised that in a few moments Seth Curtis would be dropping her off at the hotel, and with him would go her chance to find the man called Belov. She swallowed hard and said in a low voice, 'I can tell you only one thing. I'm looking for a man whose last name is Belov.' She spelled it out, pronouncing the first syllable like the word bell. 'He came to this area twenty years ago and met your father. He was planning to stay at the lodge.'

There was a fractional pause. 'I've never heard the name before,' Seth said brusquely. 'And my father died recently.'

'I know—Lily told me. I'm sorry.'

He did not acknowledge her awkward offer of sympathy. 'By the way, where am I taking you?' he asked.

'I'm staying at the same hotel as you.'

She sensed he did not like her reply. But he said nothing, turning right at the lights and then pulling up in front of White's Hotel. 'Here we are—I'll have to go and park the jeep. I'm sorry I'm not able to help you, Miss Dennis.'

It was a dismissal. She burst out, 'Surely you must have heard your father mention Belov's name? I'm certain they were friends.'

'I've already said I have never heard the name before,' Seth answered in a clipped voice.

'Then at least take me to the lodge, where I can make enquiries!'

'I don't think you quite understand. The lodge is totally isolated among hundreds of square miles of wilderness. There *is* nowhere to enquire. Unless you plan to ask the caribou or the grizzlies.'

Tascha's eyes blazed with the intensity of her purpose. 'I don't believe you! It can't be so.'

'Why are you so interested in him, anyway? Who is he?'

She told the truth. 'I don't know who he is.'

'But you've flown three thousand miles to look for him?' Seth said incredulously. 'It's my turn to disbelieve you, Miss Dennis. Look, this is a totally useless conversation. I'm sorry I'm unable to help you, and if you wish to visit the lodge next summer as a guest you'd be more than welcome. But this summer is impossible.'

She bit her lip, fighting for control. 'I'll do anything,' she pleaded. 'I'll wash dishes, I'll scrub floors—but please at least take me there!'

'No!' he exploded. 'Or isn't that a word you understand?'

It was a word she understood all too well, for it had expressed Olga's whole attitude to life. Tascha said in a thin voice, 'This is a matter of life and death to me, Mr Curtis. I'm not in the habit of begging people to do things for me—but I am begging you to take me to the lodge.'

'You will not find out anything about this man Bulov, or whatever you said his name was, at Caribou Lodge.'

Deep in Tascha's brain, a tiny signal sounded. She did not know Seth Curtis well, but she had already sensed in him an acute intelligence. He would not forget anything as simple as a name, she was sure he would not. Not to the extent of mispronouncing Belov as Bulov. Therefore he must be lying to her. He *did* know the name Belov. Every instinct in her screamed out that he knew the name.

Trying to hide her excitement, she knew she had to make one last attempt to persuade Seth to take her to the lodge, even if it meant using a weapon that could turn back on itself. Since her mid-teens she had been aware of the effect of her looks on the opposite sex, and had done her best to minimise that effect, for her attitude towards men was ambivalent, to say the least, and she had no wish to arouse passions she had no intention of satisfying. But with Seth Curtis neither reason nor anger had produced the result she wanted. Perhaps beauty would affect him, where reason had not.

So it was then that Tascha made her mistake. She leaned forward, rather wishing she had undone her rain-jacket while she was waiting at the bungalow, gazed at him through her lashes, which were every bit as long as his, and rested her fingers on his bare wrist. 'Please?' she breathed.

Beneath her fingertips she felt the clenching of muscle and tendon and the sudden surge of his pulse, and in swift triumph thought she had won. But then the initiative was seized from her. Seth twisted in his seat, dug his fingers in her hair and bent his head to kiss her. For a second that was out of time, she saw his coal-black eyes ablaze with emotion. Then his lips claimed hers and the emotion leaped to claim her too, as flames leap from treetop to treetop when the forest is on fire.

Tascha was engulfed in a primitive hunger such as she had never known before, and instinctively raised her hand to clasp his shoulders, feeling the warmth of his taut flesh under his shirt. As her hair tumbled free of its ribbon, covering his hands with the cool smoothness of silk, his kiss deepened until blindly she opened to the quick thrust of his tongue.

As if he had been waiting for this sign of her surrender, Seth pushed her away with brutal strength. His fingers were caught in her hair; she gave a tiny whimper of pain, her eyes whirlpools of blue, her hands shaking.

'You know every trick in the book, don't you?' he said harshly. 'But the answer's still no, Tascha Dennis.'

The weapon she had always feared to use had turned against her in a way she could never have anticipated; she had learned more about herself from a single kiss than she had learned from all her dates through high school and college. She had never wanted a man before, but she wanted Seth Curtis.

'I'd appreciate it if you'd get out of the jeep,' Seth suggested tersely. 'Because you're not following me up to my room.'

So had it been for him a kiss like any other? Nothing special, and she herself just another in a series of willing females? Tascha felt a hot stab of jealousy that threw her off balance as much as had her hunger, for she had never been the slightest bit jealous of anyone she had ever dated. What was happening to her? How had one man turned her whole image of herself upside-down?

She finally found her voice. 'I had no thought of following you to your room.'

'No? You said you'd do anything to get to the lodge.'

In a flash of temper she retorted, 'I didn't mean I'd sleep with you!' Five minutes ago she could have made that statement with perfect truth. Now she was not so sure.

'Oh, you figured you'd tease me a little but stop short of actual delivery?'

'There's no need to be offensive!'

'If you find the truth offensive, perhaps you should examine your actions a little more closely.'

Tascha could think of no reply to this. Her silence must have infuriated Seth, because he suddenly banged his fist on the dash. 'Will you please get out?' he snarled.

She could defend herself against the obscenities of a drunken stranger in a tavern. But against Seth's kiss she was both defenceless and mute. With some vestige of pride, she tried to keep her hand steady as she reached for the handle of the door. The door opened smoothly. She slid to the ground, the slight jar of her knees strangely reassuring. She was real, she thought. She did exist.

Not looking at Seth, she slammed the jeep door and walked towards the hotel entrance, hearing behind her the rev of the engine as he drove away. The rubber trees and the shag-pile carpet were just as they had been this afternoon. The proprietress nodded at her. 'Did you find Seth?' she asked curiously.

Tascha fought down a hysterical laugh. 'Yes, I did, thank you,' she said politely. 'Goodnight.'

She walked down the corridor to her room and unlocked the door. The room seemed like a haven, her canvas bag something familiar in a world gone awry. The digital clock on the bedside radio said eleven p.m. Two in the morning in Montreal. No wonder she was tired, she thought, deliberately closing her mind to all that had happened, knowing that her plan for the next day was already formulated.

Seth had lied to her. Seth did know something about the man called Belov. Tomorrow, if it was humanly possible, she was going to fly to the lodge and find out what he knew.

When the travel bureau opened the next morning, Tascha was standing on the steps. Although the sky was still overcast and the streets wet with rain, she was in good spirits. Seth's opposition had served to harden her resolve; despite the death of Neil Curtis, she was convinced the clues to her past were to be found at Caribou Lodge.

The young girl behind the counter gave her a bright smile. 'Can I help you?'

'I'm hoping to charter a plane to Caribou Lodge,' Tascha said, smiling back. 'Do you have any information about it?'

'I can give you one of their brochures. Do you have a reservation?'

'No, I don't. But, surely, if I arrive there, they won't turn me away?'

'Well, the main problem would be ground transportation...is this your first visit?' When Tascha nodded, the girl unfolded a map of the Yukon and indicated two points on a spidery red line that ran from Whitehorse deep into the mountains of the Northwest Territories. 'You see, the planes usually land here, at Drummond Pass. But the lodge is over here.'

'I wouldn't need to fly—I could drive all the way from Whitehorse,' Tascha said excitedly. 'I hadn't realised there was a road.'

'I wouldn't advise it. The road's in pretty good shape as far as the border, but beyond that it's not maintained, and a short distance beyond the lodge it becomes impassable.' The girl frowned. 'Your best bet is to check with Mackenzie Air and see if they have anyone else going there.'

Anyone besides Seth, thought Tascha. The red line between the airstrip and the location of the lodge was only a fraction of an inch long; was that going to stop her from completing her journey? She could not believe that it would. A road, after all, meant civilisation of a sort. 'May I take the map with me?' she asked.

'Please do. I'll give you a booklet about the Yukon, too.'

Tascha's next step was to get a cab to the hangar at the airport belonging to Mackenzie Air. She asked the taxi driver to wait for her, then pushed open the small blue door labelled with the airline's name. The door led into an office occupied by a young man in navy overalls who was talking on the phone. One whole wall was taken up by a huge map of the very area she was interested in. The road looked far more substantial than it had on the smaller map, although it was hedged in by mountains its entire length. Someone had written in the name of the lodge in pencil.

Tascha gazed at the map, seized by doubt. Why would anyone think such an isolated place a suitable home for a small child? There were no settlements for hundreds of miles, only the irregular contour lines of range after range of mountains. Rivers ran between them. White patches indicated glaciers, and she recalled Seth saying how the lodge was snowed in ten months of the year.

'Anything I can do for you?' a breezy voice said behind her.

She turned, hoping she did not look as doubtful as she felt. 'I want to go to Caribou Lodge—will you fly me there?' she said, and braced herself for almost certain refusal.

'Heading that way this afternoon if the clouds lift just a touch. Taking a guy who works for one of the outfitters—he's picking up supplies at Twin Peaks.'

Tascha looked blank. 'I thought the airstrip was at Drummond Pass.'

'Normally it is. But the radio tower's out at the border, so we can't use the landing strip at the pass.'

He seemed to take for granted that she understood what he was talking about. 'Are *you* the pilot?' she gulped.

'Yeah...been flying in the north for six years.'

He looked far too young. 'This outfitter, could I travel as far as the lodge with him?'

'Well, now, you *could*...whether you *should* is another question. Why don't you wait a day or so and go back with Seth Curtis? He runs the lodge.'

'I'd rather go today—I'm meeting someone there,' she lied.

The pilot glanced around the office. 'Look, don't quote me, will you, because we get a lot of business from the outfitters? I'd trust Eddie with a horse any day of the week. But a woman...not so sure about that.'

'You mean, we'd be travelling on horseback?'

'That's right. The outfitters are all east of the lodge. The vehicle hasn't been made that can travel that road.'

'What are the supplies for?' Tascha asked, feeling her way.

'The outfitters have camps in the mountain passes,' he explained patiently. 'Very rich people pay a whole lot of money to go in there and shoot mountain goats and caribou and Dall sheep.' His smile was malicious. 'So they can show their friends back home how clever they are.'

'Seth Curtis doesn't run that kind of place, does he?'

'Seth? Not likely! He has an ongoing feud with the outfitters because he's such a dyed-in-the-wool conservationist. He never even carries a rifle when he's tracking grizzlies.'

Increasingly, Tascha had the feeling of being totally out of her depth. Grasping the few facts that she knew, she said bluntly, 'What's wrong with Eddie?'

The young man grinned engagingly. 'If I had a daughter, which I don't, I wouldn't allow her to set off on a twenty-four-hour trek with Eddie.'

'I can handle Eddie,' Tascha said confidently, for, compared to glaciers, mountains and horses, Eddie did not seem like much of a problem. 'How much does the flight cost and when will you leave?'

The pilot raised his brows. 'Well, if you're going, take your own bedroll and your own food,' he advised. 'That way, you won't be indebted to him.'

He discussed price and departure times, and Tascha signed two traveller's cheques, inwardly appalled at the cost of a flight that lasted just over an hour. 'I'll be back here around four,' she said.

'Call first to check. If the ceiling lowers, we could run into icing. Ice on the wings,' he added casually.

'But it's July!'

'Yesterday it was zero degrees at four thousand feet. We fly between seven thousand and nine thousand feet. The plane'd drop like a chunk of lead,' he said with a cheerful grin.

His attitude was far from reassuring. Tascha managed an insincere smile. 'I'll phone first,' she promised, and went outside to the waiting cab-driver.

Tascha spent more money back in Whitehorse, buying a down sleeping-bag in a waterproof bag, a haversack and some staple items of food. Then, feeling the need to distract her mind from a journey that was beginning to seem impulsive and irrational, even to her, she went into a bookshop.

She had always loved books, some deep part of her nature drawn to the printed page, to the feel of a book in her hands, to the accumulated magic of sentence, paragraph and chapter; at university she had studied literature and mythology, her spirit soaring free of all the constrictions of her daily life. So now she deposited her parcels at the front desk and began to browse along the shelves. Eventually she decided to go through the fiction alphabetically. She had reached the Bs when the name of an author seemed to leap out at her from the neatly arranged books. Belov. The title of the book was *Treatise on Time.*

She pulled the book out, feeling the same inner trembling that Olga's two letters had caused her. She had heard the name before, of course. Andrei Belov published a novel every three or four years, receiving critical rather than popular acclaim. She had never read any of his work, and until now had not connected the name on her letters with the name of the writer.

The book looked difficult, densely written with obscure quotations heading up each chapter. But the blurb contained two sentences that riveted her eyes. 'Little is known about the author, who never grants interviews and whose personal life is shrouded in secrecy. He is believed to have emigrated from Russia about twenty years ago and to be living in the Canadian north.'

Slowly Tascha closed the cover, her blood pounding in her ears. The two letters had been sent twenty years ago.

She paid for the book, putting it carefully in her new haversack, and went back to the hotel, where she re-arranged her luggage for the flight and changed into her most comfortable jeans. Then she tucked the book under her arm and left the room, having decided that a proper lunch might be her best preparation for the expedition with Eddie. She hurried along the corridor in her soft-soled sneakers, turned a corner and walked straight into a man who had been striding in the opposite direction. As the book went flying, his arms went around her in a reflex action. She looked up and forgot all about the book. The man embracing her was Seth Curtis.

He was very much larger than she, and her first, short-lived response was one of utter security. She felt safe in the circle of his arms and found herself wishing fervently that she was going from Twin Peaks to Caribou Lodge with Seth rather than with the unreliable Eddie. But then security was ousted by a confusion of other emotions: a sensual pleasure in the strength of his arms, a wild, sweet hunger for the taut length of his body, a quite astonishing joy that by sheer chance she had seen him again. She felt his hold tighten, knew without surprise what he was going to do, and closed her eyes.

This kiss was very different from their first; it was as if Seth had felt the same emotions as she, and through his lips was telling her of hunger and of joy. She forgot that she was angry with him and forgot that she was deceiving him, for it was a kiss that spoke of truth and what could have been tenderness.

But when Seth drew back his black eyes were unfathomable; Tascha had no idea what he was thinking. 'I wasn't expecting to see you again,' he said levelly. 'How much longer are you staying in Whitehorse, Tascha?'

She told the truth, desperately unwilling to lie. 'I'm leaving this afternoon.'

His jaw tightened. 'I see. I suppose it's just as well.'

'What do you mean?'

He managed a smile which did not reach his eyes. 'First of all, I'm not in the habit of colliding with women in hotel corridors. Secondly, if by chance I do, I don't usually kiss them.'

Tascha decided to risk honesty a second time. 'I liked our second kiss much better than our first,' she said gravely.

Seth's answer was to kiss her again, this time with unquestioned tenderness and a deep passion. She was trembling when he released her, making no attempt to hide it, and could not have put into words how his third kiss had affected her. He said in a strange voice, 'You know, I've never asked you if you're married.'

She shook her head and found her tongue. 'No. I've never even had a serious boyfriend.'

'I've never been married, either.' He gave his head a sudden shake, as if to clear it. 'And don't ask me why I'm talking this way—or acting this way—because I don't know. Will you give me your address in Montreal?'

As she thought of the ugly little apartment, a shadow crossed her face. 'Yes,' she said and added without thinking, 'There's paper in my room.' Then she flushed scarlet, remembering his insinuations the night before. 'I'm not——'

'I know you're not, Tascha. You can give me the address and I'll be on my way. I'm meeting someone in half an hour.'

He was wearing soft-fitting cords and an open-necked shirt with the sleeves rolled up, quite ordinary clothes in which he looked anything but ordinary; she found herself hoping he was not going to meet a woman. Turning, she led the way back to her room, pulling the key from the pocket of her jeans, glad that her luggage was stowed away in the wardrobe, out of sight, so that he would not see her new sleeping-bag and perhaps ask awkward

questions. She was almost tempted to tell him that she
would be at the lodge when he arrived back there, but
a remnant of caution prevailed. Seth Curtis, if he chose
to, was perfectly capable of preventing her from catching
her flight.

She took a notepad from the drawer of the maple
dresser, wrote down her address and passed it to him.
He said slowly, 'Pointe Saint-Charles...we don't get
many people from there at the lodge.'

'I inherited some money,' Tascha said stiffly.

Thoughtfully his eyes ran over her off-the-rack
clothing and the patrician beauty of her face. 'You're a
mystery to me, Tascha Dennis. You look so fragile, as
though a strong wind would blow you away, and yet you
can march into the Scagway as if you owned the place.
Why have you never had a serious boyfriend?'

She was acutely aware of the passage of time, knowing
she wanted him away from the hotel when she left for
the airport, terrified that he would ask if she was returning to Montreal that afternoon. She was frightened
of something else. The bed, which was double, seemed
to her overwrought imagination to be taking up most of
the room; she wondered if Seth was as conscious of it
as she was. She had definitely not come out here to find
a lover, she scolded herself, and heard Seth say, 'You
haven't answered my question.'

She lowered her eyes. 'Oh, that's a question that would
take a very long time to answer,' she said lightly.

'And we don't have a long time.' Seth took her by the
arm. 'Tascha, look at me—may I write to you in
Montreal?'

Only wanting to be rid of him, for she hated herself
for deceiving him, Tascha babbled, 'Yes, yes, of course
you may...didn't you say you had to meet someone?'

'Do you know something? You've never called me by
my first name.'

She shivered at the intensity of his voice, feeling herself being pulled more and more deeply into the orbit of this black-haired stranger. And, because so much else between them was deception she said with absolute honesty, 'I'm not in the habit of kissing men the way I kissed you, Seth.' She gave him a quick, generous smile. 'Certainly not in hotel corridors.'

With his free hand, he stroked the curve of her cheekbone. 'Your skin is so smooth,' he marvelled. 'I——' As if words were useless, he slid his mouth down her cheek and found her lips again.

Tascha kissed him back almost with desperation, for she knew, as he did not, that the next time he saw her he would probably be extremely angry with her. His hands moved from her hair to cup her shoulders, and then travelled the length of her spine to clasp the slender curve of her waist and pull her close to him, so close that she felt his arousal and with it a knowledge of her own power.

They fell apart with a kind of mutual consent, her heart racing in her breast, his breathing harsh in his throat. 'This is ridiculous!' he rasped, glaring at her almost as if he hated her. 'I never wanted this to happen to me——'

'I never knew it *could* happen...' Tascha murmured.

But Seth did not hear her. Stepping back from her, running his fingers through his hair, he said hoarsely, 'I'm glad you're leaving. It's best. Because this is craziness! Lunacy! We don't even know each other.'

She had had time to recover. Her guilty conscience nudging her on, she said sharply, 'So go, then!'

His hands had dropped to his sides. 'I don't want to. And that's what really scares me.'

'You've got to—you'll be late.'

His eyes seemed to burn into her soul. 'Maybe in a few days I'll think I dreamed you,' he muttered, then brushed past her and slammed the door.

Tascha sat down hard on the bed, feeling as though she had been caught up in a whirlwind, tossed from side to side like a broken-winged bird and then unceremoniously dumped to the ground. Did Seth mean he'd fallen in love with her? Or did he mean he wanted to take her to bed? The latter, maybe, but surely not the former. Yesterday he had given every appearance of disliking her. So what was the craziness he talked about? What did he mean by lunacy?

Someone rapped sharply on the door. On legs that did not seem to be connected to the rest of her body, Tascha walked to the door and unlocked it, somehow not at all surprised to see that it was Seth. He was holding out the book she had bought earlier in the day, his face contorted with fury. Any trace of tenderness had vanished; he looked like the man who had threatened Slim.

'You lied to me, didn't you?' he demanded. 'You said you didn't know who Belov was—and yet you're carrying around one of his books. You'd just happened to forget that he's one of the most highly regarded writers in North America! What are you, Tascha Dennis—a reporter?'

'No, of course not,' she said in bewilderment.

'Of course not!' he repeated sarcastically. 'It would be a major scoop to run down Belov, photograph where he's living, hound him into an interview. You're not the first one to turn up in Whitehorse looking for him, and I don't suppose you'll be the last. But you'll be no more successful than any of the rest—because Belov, to the best of my knowledge, doesn't live within a thousand miles of here!'

'I am *not* a reporter!' she blazed. 'I told you my reasons for looking for him were personal.' She snatched the book out of his hands, clutching it to her breast as protectively as if it were a child. 'You lied to me, pretending you didn't even know his name.'

'Yes, I lied. And I'd lie again. Because I can't bear this twentieth-century brashness that insists it has the right to every detail of a man's life. If someone wants to live in privacy, let him—don't spread his name across the front page of every newspaper in the land.'

Tascha said with exaggerated slowness, 'I do not work for a newspaper now, I never have worked for one, and I doubt if I ever will.'

He gave a short laugh. 'You know, from the beginning I couldn't figure out the discrepancy between your face and your clothes—they just didn't match. What did you do, visit the secondhand shops on purpose?

She flushed, for some of her clothes had indeed been bought secondhand. 'These clothes happen to be all I can afford.'

'But you can fly from Montreal and charter a plane to the lodge? It's called an expense account, Tascha.'

All Tascha's confused emotions of the last half-hour dissolved into a shaft of pure rage. 'Get out of my room, Seth Curtis, and take your insinuations along with you!' she choked. 'And don't come back!'

'I won't, believe me.' He pulled the piece of paper on which she had written her address out of his pocket, crumpled it and threw it on the dresser. 'I won't be needing that, either,' he grated, and for the second time slammed the door in her face.

Tascha stamped her foot, called him every rude name she could think of in both French and English, and narrowly avoided bursting into tears. Ripping the little piece of paper into shreds made her feel slightly better. She dashed cold water on her face, which cooled her temper as well as her skin; then, defiantly carrying the book by Belov, she went to the dining-room for lunch.

She did not see Seth.

CHAPTER THREE

HAD Tascha known what lay ahead of her, she might have made an effort to appreciate her lunch more than she did. But the food tasted like cardboard, the image of Seth's furious face a barrier to any enjoyment. So he thought she was a cheap two-bit journalist looking for a sensational scoop at the price of a man's privacy, did he? He thought she was a liar. He had thrown her address in her face...but here Tascha's honesty got the better of her. He had not thrown it in her face. He had thrown it on the dresser. And she was certainly deceiving him, if not actively lying.

Glumly she ate a piece of cherry pie, not really noticing that it tasted any different from the hot turkey sandwich. She swallowed a cup of coffee. She had a horrible feeling that the lodge was probably not a large enough place that she could hide from Seth. If he had been angry with her today, he would be livid when he arrived home, to find her there before him! She remembered with dreadful clarity how he had lifted Slim by the front of Slim's checked shirt. He could pick her up with one hand. Would he throw her out on the tundra? Abandon her in a bog? Fling her into an icy mountain stream?

Tascha's imagination had always been vivid. Needing something factual to hold on to, she took out the brochure that she had been given at the tourist bureau, unfolded it and spread it out on the table. Her eyes widened with delight.

The lodge was a long, low building constructed of burnished logs, with a huge stone chimney at one end and what looked like an observation tower at the other. Tiny log cabins were clustered around it like chicks around a hen. A wide stretch of tundra lay in front of the lodge, bounded by white-capped mountains and the sky.

Her fears of Seth were pushed aside by wonderment. She wanted to stand on the little knoll in front of the lodge and look out over that vast plain to the distant mountains. She could almost hear the silence, breathe the crisp, cold air...she could not have imagined a place more different from the cramped apartment in Pointe Saint-Charles.

Quickly, Tascha glanced at her watch. She should phone the pilot. She must not miss her chance to get to the lodge ahead of Seth, particularly after seeing how beautiful it was. After paying her bill, she went back to her room and dialled the number of the airline.

'Galvin Pearce. Mackenzie Air.'

'It's Tascha Dennis speaking. Are you still leaving at four?'

'C'mon out right now. We'll be ready to leave in half an hour.'

Tascha rang off, checked out of the hotel and took a taxi to the hangar, and the whole time a vision of the mountains danced in front of her eyes. She paid the cab-driver, then, taking a deep breath, she pushed open the blue door to Mackenzie Air.

The office was empty. Tascha took a quick glance at the map, remembering how its impersonal orange and green contours had been translated into glorious reality by a single photograph, and stepped through a second door into the hangar. Galvin, the pilot, was standing by a baggage cart, talking earnestly to a bow-legged man in high-heeled boots and a stetson, who looked over at

Tascha as she entered the hangar. A little of Tascha's euphoria evaporated, for the man would not have been miscast as one of the villains in the cowboy movies she used to go to on Saturday afternoon when she was a little girl.

She drew herself to her full height, trying to look capable, pleasant and unapproachable all at the same time, and walked across the concrete floor towards the two men. Galvin called out, 'Hi there, Tascha! Meet Eddie Smith. Eddie, this is Tascha Dennis. I told you about her.'

Eddie did not raise his hat or offer to shake hands. He looked her over from head to foot, a little as if she were a heifer he was thinking of bidding on, and said, 'You plannin' on travellin' with me?'

'As far as the lodge,' said Tascha.

'We'll likely camp over.'

Recalling Galvin's term, she said, 'I've got a bedroll.'

He gave a brief nod, as though something had been settled to his satisfaction. 'Know how to ride?'

'No. But I can learn.'

'Those old nags of yours won't give any trouble,' Galvin joked. 'Is that all your gear, Tascha?' She nodded. 'OK, we might as well load up and get going.' Hoisting a couple of well worn saddlebags from the cart, he led the way towards the door of the hangar.

Tascha decided she should at least make an effort to be friendly to Eddie. He could not be held responsible for his eyes being set too close together, or even for his bad teeth; trying to ignore the dark stubble on his chin and the greasy hair under the stetson, things for which he *was* responsible, she said, 'It's kind of you to take me to the lodge.'

Eddie gave her an enigmatic look and grunted something under his breath. Then he picked up two heavily loaded haversacks as easily as if they were paper bags, and followed Galvin out of the hangar.

Tascha pulled a face. However, it suited her fine if Eddie didn't want to be friendly; she could put up with anything for twenty-four hours in order to reach the lodge.

A very small plane was parked outside the hangar. It was like a toy plane built from a kit, Tascha thought whimsically, right down to its orange and white paint, and she looked around for the plane they would be using. But Galvin had dumped the saddlebags under the wing of the orange plane and was opening its door; the plane was the same height as he. She blurted, 'Are we flying in *that*?'

'Sure.' He grinned at her. 'Cessna Stationair Six II. Great little plane.' He climbed inside and took the luggage from Eddie, storing it in the back.

The propellers, which were supposed to carry them through the sky, were about the length of Galvin's arms. There were neat black stripes between the orange paint on the fuselage and the white. Orange so they would show up should they crash, Tascha thought sickly.

'You get in first,' said Galvin.

Suppressing an urge to kneel and kiss the concrete, Tascha did as she was told, folding herself into a seat that was surprisingly comfortable. Eddie and Galvin took the two front seats, Galvin pulling the door shut and casually latching it. Then he checked a few dials, started the engine, put on a head-set and began a low-voiced conversation.

Eddie not only looked dirty, he smelled dirty, Tascha quickly discovered. The plane started taxiing from the hangar to the runway. After Galvin had done another quick check, they began speeding along the runway, faster and faster, until smoothness replaced the bumps and Tascha realised with a lurch of her heart that they were airborne. The hangars and the control tower were left behind. Beneath her, the city of Whitehorse gradually diminished to tidy rows of buildings along a winding grey-green ribbon, and then disappeared through the clouds.

'Might be a little rough here,' Galvin called out. 'Keep your seat-belt on.'

For the next half-hour Tascha concentrated on keeping her hot turkey sandwich and cherry pie where they belonged. The staggers and dips and sudden drops of the Cessna terrified her; she counted the number of ridges in the tyres and memorised the pattern of chipping paint on the strut nearest the door. They were flying just above the clouds, through which, occasionally, the black peaks of mountains coyly poked. These reminders of terra firma did not reassure Tascha.

However, when the cloud cover eventually thinned, the plane flew more smoothly, and through the wisps of white below her Tascha could see Galvin's map made real. Mountains heaved up from the ground, their gaunt grey flanks streaked with ice, the green valleys between them crinkled by pale blue creeks. She saw the silver of lakes and rivers, the dark green of the low-flung spruce forests, the dirty white of last winter's snow. And always the mountains, range after range of them, stretching in all directions until they blended, blue-hazed, into the clouds. She was filled with awe because the mountains were beautiful, and with fear because they were harsh and black and hostile to man, and because she, Tascha Dennis, was ignorant of the rules of this wild, vast land.

They flew for over an hour, then the sound of the engine changed as Galvin began his descent, taking the plane between the peaks towards low hills covered with spruce trees. The runway was a short gravelled break in the trees. Tascha closed her eyes.

She did not open them until after the plane had bumped on the runway and Galvin called out, 'Here we are! Twin Peaks. Dawson Mountain to your left, Mount Harmony ahead. This way, please, ladies and gentlemen.'

He was obviously expecting her to laugh. She managed a weak smile. A transport truck, a black jeep, a pile of oil drums and an orange-painted building with a radio antenna were the only signs of civilisation at the airstrip. But the sun was shining and there were tall rose-pink flowers massed along the edge of the runway. Tascha climbed out of the plane and once again was on solid ground; she was sure she would never take it for granted again.

The next two hours passed slowly. Galvin unloaded the gear, shook Tascha's hand and took off with as little ceremony as he had landed. She watched the Cessna until it became a tiny dot that merged into the clouds, knowing in her inner heart that she wanted to run after it, yelling to Galvin that she had changed her mind. The mosquitoes had descended on her as soon as she had left the plane; she had not thought to buy insect repellent. Maybe that was why Eddie stayed dirty, she thought wryly—in self-protection. She had offered to help him, had met with a dour refusal, and had been left to swat the mosquitoes while he led several small horses from the truck, harnessed them and fastened packs to their backs. She ate a nut bar, scratched her bites, and tried not to think about Seth.

It was a relief to start off. Tascha was riding a sturdy brown mare whose name was Dolly and who seemed placidly indifferent to Tascha's ineptitude. The western saddle was comfortable, and Dolly's sway-backed stride very peaceful after the Cessna's ups and downs; Tascha began to enjoy herself. Besides, every step was a step nearer the lodge. She admired the cone-shaped rise of Dawson Mountain and the huge, pocketed glaciers of

Mount Harmony; over the creak of leather and the crunch of hooves on the gravel road she could discern the immense silence of the wilderness, a silence little changed in thousands of years. She drifted into a trance, proud of herself for being where she was. Initiative was all it took to outwit the Seth Curtises of this world, she thought dreamily. She had really been rather clever...

Two and a half hours later, Tascha was not quite so convinced of her own cleverness. The western saddle had transformed itself into an instrument of torture and Dolly's plodding gait into a source of agony. She was sure that her knees and thighs were rubbed raw under the seams of her jeans; she knew without a doubt that every muscle from waist to ankle ached. If she survived the next few hours she would look at jockeys and cowboys with new eyes, she thought fuzzily. They were heroes. Men of steel.

Eddie, who was riding ahead of her with a haversack and rifle slung on his back, had not budged in the saddle since they had started out. He smoked a series of foul-smelling cigars and ignored her completely. To add to her misery, her stomach was growling and she was extremely thirsty. They had crossed several creeks, all boiling with crystal-clear water, but it was a feat beyond her capabilities to dismount, hold on to Dolly, drink and remount. She knew her limits.

Imperceptibly, it began to grow dark. But another hour passed before Eddie shouted a gruff command and led the horses down a side track, to where a creek had widened into a pond which was surrounded by patches of coarse grass. The horses began to whicker, and Dolly, with more interest than she had shown all afternoon, yanked her head down to eat, almost unseating her rider.

Eddie busied himself unloading the horses and hob-bling them together. Very carefully, Tascha eased her feet out of the stirrups, debating which way of dismounting was liable to cause her the least pain. She settled for leaning forward over the horn, bringing one leg behind her and then sliding to the ground. Once there, she clutched the stirrup leathers. Her knees felt like jelly. The rest of her seemed to be on fire. She fought back tears of pain, determined that Eddie should not see them, and wondered if she would ever be able to walk again.

Dolly took two steps forward, angling for a particularly luxuriant clump of grass. Tascha staggered forward as well, still holding grimly to the stirrup. Her legs worked, she thought, light-headed with pain. Hurray, hurray! Now bring on the three-course dinner and the sauna bath.

Over his shoulder, Eddie tossed a laconic command at her. 'You kin start a fire. There's stew in that bag.' He indicated the haversack to which the rifle was strapped, then turned back to the horses.

Very gingerly, Tascha leaned the rifle against a tree. Inside the bag she found a big jar of stew, a blackened cooking pot and some matches. The camp site had been used before, because there was a circle of stones from other fires. Stooping awkwardly, she gathered kindling and some bigger pieces of wood. It took three attempts to light the kindling, because it was green, and her clumsy arrangement of the wood caused Eddie to spit very accurately into its smouldering centre and mutter, 'Don't you know nuthin'?'

She took it for a rhetorical question and watched humbly as he coaxed crackling flames and warmth where she had produced only smoke. The stew was eaten with chunks of coarse bread and tasted delicious, although Tascha wisely did not enquire what kind of meat it contained. Eddie then made coffee in a battered pot, and took a bottle of whiskey from his bag. He unscrewed it, took a long pull, wiped his mouth, and passed the bottle to her. 'Want some?'

It was his first friendly gesture. While she would not have admitted it, Tascha was finding the slow accretion of darkness frightening, for the mountains now looked like jagged, blackened teeth against the horizon, the shrubs were full of strange rustlings, and the light of the fire seemed to make the darkness all the more threatening. Hoping she was not committing a breach of etiquette, she scrubbed the lip of the bottle on her shirt, and took a mouthful of the amber liquid.

It burned its way down her throat. She sputtered, wiped involuntary tears from her eyes and passed the bottle back. 'Thanks.'

'You kin wash the dishes in the creek. Don't want to attract grizzlies.' Eddie tipped back his head and took another long swallow.

'Grizzlies?' Tascha faltered.

'Sure—this is grizzly country. My partner got mauled by one, a big sow, not three miles from here. Took half the skin off his back, she did.'

The rustlings in the undergrowth took on a greater menace. Eddie's tiny eyes gleamed maliciously in the dancing flames.

'You never seen a grizzly?' he asked.

'No. I come from the city.'

'Figured that.' He jerked his head. 'Scour the plates with sand, gets rid of the grease.'

Tascha did not feel the time was appropriate for a lecture on women's liberation; and Eddie had, after all, provided the stew. The water in the creek was ice-cold. Her hands and wrists numb, Tascha scrubbed the plates clean enough to discourage any grizzly, and stumbled back to the fire. Eddie had spread out a bedroll on the ground. 'Might as well turn in,' he said. 'You git in first.'

She looked at him without comprehension. 'Oh, I've got my own sleeping-bag,' she said.

He leered at her. 'No sense usin' two. Warmer with one.'

Unease sharpened her voice. 'No, that's OK. I'd rather use my own.'

The leer vanished. 'Git in there,' he said. 'What d'you figure I brought you along for?'

Tascha edged away from the fire. 'Come on, Eddie, the joke's over,' she said. 'I'll put my bag on the other side of the fire.'

His hand suddenly shot out and seized her wrist. 'I'd rather you were willin', but it don't make much difference either way. I did ask you, remember? I said we got to camp over and you said OK.'

'I didn't know what you meant or I wouldn't have come with you. Let go of my arm, Eddie, you're hurting!'

He dropped her wrist. 'Well, you know now. Move it, we gotta make an early start in the mornin'.'

One part of her found it screamingly funny that two people could communicate so differently; the other part was terrified. 'I've got to go and wash first,' she said.

'Hurry up, then—I ain't got all night.'

If she once started laughing she would not be able to stop. Cautiously, Tascha circled away from him round the fire. Then she lunged for the tree near his bag, picked up the rifle and said breathlessly, 'I'm not going to sleep with you, Eddie.'

He was on his feet in a flash, his face contorted with fury. 'You put that down!'

She felt much better with the smooth wood of the stock against her palm. 'I don't have a clue how to use this thing,' she admitted, 'but if you come one step closer, I'll make a darn good try.'

Something in her face kept Eddie standing where he was. He began cursing her, a stream of words that made her feel dirty and degraded; but she kept her hand steady on the rifle and her eyes glued to the man on the other side of the fire. His last words were, 'Don't you figure on ridin' no horse of mine tomorrow—you kin walk the rest of the way.' He sat down on the bedroll, pulled off his boots, put his stetson carefully beside them, and got inside the sleeping-bag. Ostentatiously, he turned his back on her and the fire.

For a full five minutes Tascha stayed where she was. Eddie began to snore, long wheezes that she was almost sure were genuine. Almost, but not quite. She stood for another five minutes, feeling rather foolish, glad that only the horses could see her so eloquently defending her virtue. But then she would remember the venom in Eddie's eyes and her hands would tighten on the gun.

Her bedroll was only two feet from Eddie's head. Knowing she lacked the courage to get it, she slowly backed away from the fire. There was a screen of bushes between her and the creek; if she tucked herself among them she would be out of Eddie's sight yet near enough to the fire for protection against marauding grizzlies. She hoped.

Tascha had never spent a more uncomfortable night in all her twenty-two years than the one she spent perched on a rock, with her back against the narrow trunk of a poplar and with the creek rushing in her ears. The horses shifted and nickered. Eddie snored. She occasionally drifted off to sleep herself, only to be gripped by a nightmare and startled to wakefulness, her heart pounding over the splash and rattle of the creek.

The northern summer nights are short, and for that Tascha was very grateful. As the cool grey light of dawn brought green back to the leaves of the poplars and brown to Dolly's flanks, Tascha relaxed a little. She was dozing, the rifle loosely held across her knees, when a twig snapped and jerked her awake. Eddie was standing ten feet away from her.

'Get back!' she quavered and pointed the rifle at him.

He said viciously, 'I'm gettin' outa here. Hope you like walkin'.'

Her eyes were burning with sleeplessness and her fingers trembling with cold. From her hideaway in the bushes, she watched him rekindle the fire, on which he then cooked bacon and pancakes, and boiled coffee. They all smelled delicious. She knew better than to ask for any.

Ignoring her as if she did not exist, Eddie cleaned up the campsite, strapped the saddlebags on the horses, including Dolly, and mounted the grey gelding he had ridden yesterday. He shouted something that sounded like 'Hi-yup!' The horses ambled up the slope towards the road. He had left Tascha's sleeping-bag and haversack beside the circle of blackened stones.

Terrified of being left alone, Tascha ducked clear of the bushes, still clutching the rifle. Every muscle she possessed screamed in protest. She splashed cold water from the creek on her face and had a long drink, took two nut bars from her haversack and tied the bedroll to it, then heaved the whole thing on her back. Moving as quickly as she could, she headed for the road.

The vista was magnificent, for she was in a wide green-carpeted valley flanked by huge mountains which were patched with ice and snow, over which the sky hovered, a clear pale blue. Ahead of her she could see the road meandering through the valley; it was edged with the same tall pink flowers she had noticed at the airstrip. But the beauty of the view did not hold Tascha's attention for long. Eddie and the packtrain were already some distance ahead of her, for Eddie was moving the horses along at a trot. She felt a sudden boil of anger. Eddie intended to leave her behind. She'd see about that.

She began walking as fast as she could, chewing on the first nut bar as she went. In the early morning light Eddie's talk of grizzlies seemed fantastical, a ruse to frighten her into his sleeping-bag. Her muscles began to loosen up. The sun warmed her cheek. This was an adventure, she thought buoyantly, and ate the second nut bar.

As the morning stretched on, however, Tascha found it difficult to maintain a sense of adventure, for pragmatic, physical concerns gradually ousted it. Her sneakers were not built for long-distance hiking on rough gravel roads; her jeans were rubbing the sore patches of her legs; the weight of her haversack was causing a stabbing pain between her shoulder-blades; and, worst of all, Eddie was slowly but surely drawing away from her. The mountains, which earlier had seemed so beautiful, now increased her sense of unease, for compared to them she was a tiny speck in the wilderness, a creature of no significance. Walking by herself on a Montreal street she had never felt lonely; here she felt paralysingly alone, as though she were the inhabitant of a dream landscape who could vanish if the sleeper stirred. She tried singing and whistling, partly to reassure herself of her own reality, partly to break the silence that seemed to throb against her ears. Then she lost sight of Eddie completely as the road wound down a hill. She found herself running up the next slope, searching for him frantically when she reached the top, but only minimally reassured when she saw him. Before long he *would* be out of sight. And she had no idea how far she was from the lodge.

For another mile the road went up and down a series of low hills that were blanketed with pale yellow lichen and dotted with green shrubs. Blisters on her heels added

themselves to Tascha's misery; she held fast to her grati-
tude that the mosquitoes appeared to have been left
behind at Twin Peaks, and by way of distraction picked
one of the tall pink flower stems that grew by the
roadside.

Each flower in the cluster was beautifully made, the
petals veined and translucent. Tascha tramped along,
crossing a bridge over a creek, knowing she had never
taken the time to look so closely at a flower before. Not
very many grew around the apartment in Pointe Saint-
Charles.

The road climbed again from the creek bed. Trying
to ease the haversack into a different position on her
back, she glanced up. Suddenly, her feet stopped dead.
Her heart gave a single loud thump, then began to race
in her breast like the beat of a bird's wing.

Two large animals were silhouetted against the sky at
the crest of the hill.

For a split second of sheer, atavistic terror, Tascha
thought they were grizzlies. But they were a pale beige
colour, and even she knew grizzlies were brown.
Mountain lions? Then, with another leap of her pulse,
she arrived at the truth. Wolves. A pair of wolves was
between her and Eddie.

The Big Bad Wolf and Little Red Riding Hood raced
through her brain. She had no idea wolves were so large.
Larger than any dog she had ever seen. And discon-
certingly interested in her.

Tascha took two steps backwards. The foremost wolf
took four steps towards her. The one behind sniffed the
air, its ears pricked, its features, even at that distance,
marked by a formidable intelligence.

Tascha retreated again. Both wolves began trotting
down the hill. With the confused notion of delaying
them, Tascha dragged her haversack off her back and
dropped it to the ground, along with Eddie's rifle, which

it never occurred to her to use. In her panic, still clutching the flower stem, she pivoted, thudded across the wooden bridge and ran back up the hill in a spurt of speed she would not have thought herself capable of. She glanced over her shoulder. The wolves were still following her.

More frightened then she had ever been in her life, she topped the hill, charged down the next one, her legs and arms flailing the air, and began climbing again. Her breath was tearing at her throat. Her legs felt like bars of lead. She risked looking over her shoulder again, and then with the crazy logic of a nightmare heard the squeal of brakes and the rip of gravel and felt something long and black brush her body. She lost her balance, falling heavily to her knees, tiny stones digging into her palms.

A door slammed. A man's voice cried, 'My God! *Tascha*...did I hit you?' Then she was being hauled roughly to her feet.

The man was Seth.

CHAPTER FOUR

TASCHA burst into tears.

She felt Seth's arms go hard around her. 'Did I hurt you? For God's sake, answer me!'

Sobbing hysterically, she burrowed her face into his chest and held on for dear life. He was safety. He was security. He was solid and warm and real and she never wanted to let go.

A hand levered her chin up. 'Tascha, stop that crying!'

The command in his voice was belied by the fear and uncertainty in his black eyes. She gave one last hiccuping sob and gasped, rather foolishly, 'I'm OK.'

He let go of her chin to grip her shoulders. 'I came over the hill, and there you were in the middle of the road,' he said raggedly. 'I jammed on the brakes, but the jeep skidded and I thought I'd hit you. My God, if I had...' Like a man possessed, he bent his head and kissed her.

She clung to him, losing herself in his kiss, knowing with the kind of elemental truth that comes only rarely in a lifetime that she was exactly where she wanted to be. In Seth's arms, hearing his voice desperately mutter her name between kisses, feeling the demand of his lips, the infinite comfort of his embrace. He would keep her safe from wolves and mountains, from loneliness and fear... he would waken her body to joy.

Then his searching fingers probed the sore spot between her shoulders and she gave a yelp of pain. He pulled free. 'What's wrong? Was it Eddie—did he hurt you? Is that why you were running away?'

Her laugh was a little wild. 'Oh, no, these were real wolves.'

He frowned. 'What are you talking about?'

'There are two wolves over the next hill—they were chasing me. That's why I was running.'

'If they heard the jeep, they'll be long gone,' Seth said impatiently. 'Anyway, I can't imagine they'd be chasing you.'

'I didn't stop to ask,' she quavered. 'When they started down the hill towards me, I ran in the opposite direction.' She added, thinking he would congratulate her for her cleverness, 'But I left my pack behind to delay them.'

'You *what*?' he thundered. 'Did it have food in it?'

'Well, yes. But——'

The only emotion in Seth's eyes now was anger. 'That's the worst thing you could have done! That's what gets wild animals into trouble, associating humans with food. Why do you think the grizzlies at Jasper and Banff are so much of a problem? Because ignorant tourists like you think it's cute to feed them!'

'Oh,' Tascha muttered, totally deflated. 'I didn't realise...'

'You didn't realise?' he repeated with heavy sarcasm. 'Do you think ignorance is an excuse? Get in the jeep— we'll go and get it right now.'

The jeep that had so nearly run her down was the one that had been parked at Twin Peaks. Tascha climbed in awkwardly, conscious of a leaden depression. Whenever she and Seth got within ten feet of each other they started to fight, she thought miserably. Or kiss. She was not sure which disturbed her more.

With the rifle angled across it, her haversack was still lying in the middle of the road. There was no sign of the wolves. Seth picked up the bag and threw it in the back of the jeep. 'Whose gun?' he demanded.

'Eddie's.'

There was no softening of his face. 'You'd better tell me what happened. The reason I'm here is because Galvin let it drop that you'd flown in with Eddie. Galvin might be a great pilot, but he's a damn fool to have allowed you to do that.'

'He did warn me.'

'But you, of course, paid no attention.' His eyes were cold. 'Tell me how you got Eddie's gun, Tascha.'

As briefly and colourlessly as she could, she related the events of yesterday evening and the morning. 'So I've been walking ever since,' she concluded. 'Until I saw the wolves. When, as you saw, I started running.'

He did not smile. 'Why have you got those on your feet?'

'My sneakers?' she said, surprised. 'They're all I've got.'

'What do you think this is?' he exploded. 'A city park? Mont Royal? This is the wilderness, Tascha. The north. Sure, it looks like a picture postcard today, blue sky and pink flowers and pretty mountains—but this country can kill you. It's harsh and unforgiving and, unless you know how to take it on its own terms, you can get into serious trouble. To start with, no one heads up here without a decent pair of hiking boots. That's basic, for God's sake!'

She bit her lip, knowing he was right, hating him for being so right. 'It will no doubt please you, then, that my sneakers have given me blisters,' she said sarcastically.

A wintry smile crossed his face. 'And I bet you haven't had any breakfast.'

'Eddie cooked bacon, pancakes and coffee. Enough for one.'

'We'll park by the creek and I'll make tea. The wolves, by the way, were almost certainly just curious about you. In all my years in the north, I've never heard of a wolf attacking a human.'

Remembering her terrified flight, Tascha ducked her head in shame. Seth drove to the creek and jumped out of the jeep. Tascha fumbled with the door-handle; she was feeling the effects of her run, none of which were pleasant, and was hoping Seth would busy himself with the food so she could ease herself to the ground very slowly without being seen. But Seth opened the door and grabbed her hand to help her get down. Unprepared, she fell forward. The heels of her sneakers caught at her blisters; the road jarred her sore knees unbearably. Her sharp, indrawn breath and sudden pallor made Seth exclaim, 'The jeep did hit you!'

She shook her head, trying to make a joke out of pain that had brought tears to her eyes. 'I've never been on a horse before yesterday—I'm sore all over.'

His eyes narrowed. 'It's not just that, Tascha.'

He was holding her by the elbows and she knew quite well that he would not release her until he was satisfied with her answer. 'The jeep didn't touch me, truly,' she said. 'You must be a very good driver. I think I lost some skin off my legs yesterday, that's all.'

'OK,' Seth said grimly. 'There's a first-aid kit in the back of the jeep. We'll go down by the creek and you can roll up your trousers and we'll take a look.'

She thought it best to obey, to try and keep on his good side. He had said nothing yet about their eventual destination; for all she knew, Galvin could be waiting for them at Twin Peaks to fly her back to Whitehorse. She stumbled down the bank, trampling on the white flowers that crowded to the very edge of the stream. 'What are those called?' she asked. 'And the pink flowers that grow along the road?'

'These are cloudberry—the fruit is edible. The pink ones are fireweed. They're the territorial flower of the Yukon. Sit on that rock and take off your sneakers—if you've got blisters, it won't hurt to soak your feet in the stream.'

Tascha had once been described by an elementary teacher as better led than driven; in other words, she disliked taking orders. She discovered she particularly disliked taking Seth's orders, even when they made good sense. But she could not afford to alienate him more than she already had. She sat down on a rock near the creek, was wincingly reminded of the rock on which she had spent the night, and took off her sneakers. Her socks were stuck to her heels. Hurriedly, she submerged her feet in the water, socks and all.

With the same easy confidence she had admired in Eddie, Seth had started a fire. As the flames crackled and spat, something tight-held in Tascha slowly relaxed. Despite all that had happened and could still happen, she felt safe with Seth and very happy to be with him.

He filled a billycan in the stream and hung it on a metal tripod over the fire. Taking some packages out of a canvas bag, he said economically, 'Turkey sandwiches, corned beef sandwiches and fruitcake. Let me see your feet, Tascha.'

The cold water had deadened all feeling in them. She lifted them back on the land and watched in silence as Seth carefully stripped off her socks. The blisters had broken.

'I'll have to put dressings on them,' he said evenly. 'You won't be able to wear your sneakers for a couple of days. Now let's see your knees.'

But her jeans were too tight at the cuff to roll up to her knees. She spoke as evenly as he had. 'They're fine, I'm sure.'

He said with overdone patience, 'There are no doctors up here, Tascha, so you can't risk infection. Take off your trousers—I've got an antibiotic cream in the kit.'

'In broad daylight?' she squeaked.

'There's no one here to see you,' he said drily.

Except you, thought Tascha, no longer feeling quite so safe. Earlier, the wilderness had threatened her with a sense of isolation; now that she was not alone, the threat had changed. 'Give me the cream,' she suggested. 'I can look after myself.'

Seth raised one eyebrow. 'You'll forgive me for doubting that. Look, I'm not trying to pull an Eddie on you—trust me. Getting sick up here can be one hell of a problem, and I've had a fair bit of experience in first-aid over the years.'

He spoke so sensibly and so rationally that Tascha would have felt foolish to protest. 'Turn your back,' she said, and unzipped her jeans, sliding them down her hips. Her shirt was a man's shirt bought in a used clothing outlet; the tails came down past her hips. The inner curve of each knee was rubbed raw, and there were angry red patches on her thighs.

Seth had turned around. He said flatly, 'You managed to run with your legs in that shape?'

'I was very frightened,' she admitted ruefully; not for the first time, she had no idea what he was thinking.

'Sit on that rock. I'll put dressings on your knees to protect them.'

He opened a wooden box, quickly extracting what he needed. The antibiotic cream was cool and soothing, and his touch very gentle. Tascha watched his hands in fascination. His fingers were long and tanned, the nails well kept; under the dark hair on the backs of his hands she could see the controlled play of muscle and tendon. She was disarmed by his gentleness, and shocked to discover that she liked the brush of his fingers on her flesh; although liked was a wholly inadequate word for the lick of flame that seemed to sear its way along her thigh. She could feel herself blushing and was helpless to prevent the heat that crept up her throat and scorched her cheeks. She bent her head, staring at the rocky soil as if nothing else in the world was of interest. Then she heard Seth say her name, his quiet voice somehow cutting through the clamour of the creek. She looked up.

His face was taut with a mixture of emotions she could not possibly have defined, his black eyes depthless. He said, more to himself than to her, 'Why do you affect me so strongly? There's something about you . . . I can't seem to help myself.'

She thought he was going to kiss her, and would have welcomed it. Instead, he lowered his hand. She watched, her nerves quivering, as with one finger he traced a blue vein along the creamy skin of her thigh. 'I've never wanted to touch a woman the way I want to touch you,' he muttered. 'It's as though I'm discovering what a woman is... Why do you do this to me?' There was sudden anger in his voice. 'What is it about you? You've lied to me and deceived me—I don't even *like* you!'

The pain this time was different, attacking the innermost core of Tascha's being, the part she had always sworn she would keep to herself. Yet this man with the raven-black hair had reached that core, unbeknown to her; her vulnerability horrified her as much as his words had hurt her. Desperate to protect herself, she lashed out at him. 'You're really just a more sophisticated version of Eddie, Seth—admit it. You want me physically—I presume that's the message—but you're not interested in me as a person.'

He drew back sharply, as if a snake had struck at him. 'So that's how you see it.'

'What other way is there?'

Visibly she could see him retreat from her. 'Perhaps you're right,' he said with an indifference that almost rang true. His movements precise and impersonal, he picked up gauze pads and covered the raw patches on her knees with them, then taped the pads neatly into place. 'That should do,' he said, not meeting her eyes. 'I'll make the tea.'

Had she followed her bent she would have flung the first-aid kit at his back. But this was a place, she was starting to realise, where one treated first-aid kits with respect. She gave a philosophical sigh, taped up her blisters, limped up to the jeep to get some dry socks, and appropriated a pair of very large rubber boots that she found there.

The sandwiches looked delicious. Finding a patch of lichen to cushion her behind, Tascha sat down and began to eat. Silently Seth passed her a mug of tea.

Tascha ate and drank with serious pleasure. In the sunlight, the white flowers of the cloudberry shone like little stars among their dark green foliage. The creek burbled to itself. High overhead, a bird drifted into view, wings outspread as it effortlessly soared on invisible air currents. Forgetting that she was angry with Seth, Tascha said, 'Is that an eagle?'

He looked up. 'An immature golden eagle. There are white patches on its wings that the adult lacks.'

She said dreamily, 'How wonderful to be so free.'

'You're romanticising, Tascha. Like the rest of us, an eagle has to eat and find shelter and mate.'

She considered him thoughtfully, in a flash of insight understanding him a little better, this man who was unlike any other she had ever known. He, like the eagle, fitted this landscape. He was at home in it, respecting it without being incapacitated by it. And there was something elemental about his use of the word mate...would Seth Curtis choose his woman instinctively, unable to help himself? Tascha was filled with a strange excitement. But on the heels of excitement fear followed quickly, for she had no idea what his plans were for her. If he took her back to Twin Peaks, he would ensure she would not be allowed to return to the lodge.

She would never see him again. And this wild, beautiful country would become nothing but a dream.

Seth said prosaically, 'More tea?'

'No, thanks.' Without finesse, Tascha said, 'I suppose we'll have supper at the lodge.'

Very deliberately, he dumped the contents of the billy-can on the fire, dousing the flames. The ashes hissed demoniacally. 'What makes you think I'm taking you to the lodge?' he said.

In a rush of adrenalin, Tascha knew she was fighting for her life, and could not have said who was the more important—the man called Belov or the man squatting three feet from her, his eyes avoiding hers. She said calmly, 'You won't leave me here; you have too much sense of responsibility for that.'

'How well you know me,' he said ironically. 'You're a born manipulator, aren't you?'

She refused to back down. 'A realist,' she said.

'Realist enough to know, then, that I can drive you to the airstrip and put you on the plane for Whitehorse.'

'You'd have to tie me hand and foot,' Tascha said gently. 'Because I won't go willingly.'

He was looking at her now, all the force of his personality in his gaze. 'A declaration of war, Tascha?'

'We declared war back in Whitehorse when I asked you to take me to the lodge and you refused.'

'So we did. Your tactics have been less than honourable.'

She flushed, for his contempt was only thinly veiled. 'I'd come a long way. I couldn't allow you to stop me.'

'You will not find the famous Andrei Belov at the lodge, Tascha,' Seth said calmly. 'Use your head—all the other guests would know who he was and the secret would be out in no time. You're on the wrong track. Even if he does live somewhere in the north, you haven't got a hope of finding him, it's too immense an area. Save your money and go home.'

If Seth was angry with her, he was keeping it well hidden; he merely sounded reasonable, even concerned. Tascha stared at him in silence, assailed by doubts, for what was she going on but intuition and two letters written twenty years ago? Andrei Belov, the writer, might not even be the Belov she sought; and because she so desperately wanted to be freed of Olga, she could be deluding herself to see any connection between herself and the letter-writer and his beloved Marya... She was Olga's daughter, daughter of a woman who had not loved her. She would never know her father, for that secret had died with Olga. As Seth had so succinctly put it, she should go home and save her money. She was on the wrong track, a track that led nowhere but into a wilderness of the spirit.

'Don't look like that!' Seth said sharply.

Her blue eyes were dazed, as though she were lost in a vast forest and no longer had the resolve to seek a way out; under the warm sun, she was shivering. She suddenly buried her face in her hands. 'You're right—you'd better take me back. I've been a fool,' she whispered. 'I should never have come here.' She should have bundled Olga's meagre belongings into a box and given them away; she should not have gone through them and read the letters. Then she would never have found this land of silence and vaulted skies where eagles soared. She would never have met a black-haired man whose touch was magic and whose kisses pierced her to the soul.

'I can't take you back,' Seth said in a voice devoid of emotion. 'Galvin had to go back to Whitehorse to fly some oilmen up to Inuvik.'

Better never to have met him than to be forced to leave him and go thousands of miles away and never see him again...

'Tascha, did you hear me?'

She lowered her hands, gazing at him blankly. 'What?'

'I can't take you back to Twin Peaks,' Seth said, speaking as slowly and clearly as he would have to a small child. 'Galvin's gone. You'll have to come to the lodge with me.'

'But you don't want me there!'

'I don't have much choice, do I?'

Tascha stared down at the rounded toes of the big black boots, wanting to burst into tears for the second time that day, and said with unconscious pathos, 'I'm so tired of not being wanted.'

She was hunched up on the rock, her feet looking ludicrously large in his boots, her blonde head bowed. Seth said urgently, 'Tell me why you're looking for Belov, why it's so important to you. Then I'll understand.'

Belov was a mirage in the desert, a wish-fulfilment, a creation of her own needs. She shook her head. 'I'm not looking for him any more,' she said dully. 'He's no longer important.'

'I wish I could believe you.'

'I've been such a fool...'

Seth gave a frustrated sigh. 'We'd better go. I want to get home for dinner.'

Slowly she looked up. 'How long will I stay?'

'There's a flight on Sunday. One set of guests leaves and a new group arrives.'

Four days. Tascha picked up the first-aid kit and her sneakers and hobbled up the bank. Then she curled up in the passenger seat, using her jacket as a pillow, and closed her eyes. She did not want to talk to Seth. She did not want to think about Belov. She did not want to be haunted by the beauty of an unattainable land.

'Tascha, wake up!'

A hand was shaking her shoulder. Eddie, Tascha thought confusedly. Eddie had found her... as her eyes flew open, she raised an arm to ward him off and looked straight into Seth's face. 'Oh,' she said stupidly, 'it's you.'

He said shrewdly, 'Eddie really frightened you, didn't he? You'll be glad to know we passed him an hour back.'

'Where are we now?' The jeep was parked among a group of roughly built sheds that were painted a variety of colours.

'This is a tungsten mine near the border. Non-operational for the past three or four years. An old fellow named Hans lives here from May until October to prevent any vandalism.'

Tascha was more fully awake now. She looked around her. 'The landscape doesn't seem to be crowded with potential vandals.'

Seth laughed. 'You'd be surprised...Hans loves company, so I always call in. He'll make you a cup of coffee that'll take the roof off your mouth, he'll insist you eat a piece of pie, and he'll probably propose to you before you leave.'

It was Tascha's turn to laugh. 'But I'm not to take it as a compliment because he proposes to every female who comes along, right?'

'Got it.'

Hans was only a couple of inches taller than Tascha; his beard and snow-white hair would have shamed many a department-store Santa Claus, as would his smile. 'Seth, my old friend,' he boomed. 'I go to put the coffee-pot on. And who is this?' He looked appreciatively at Tascha.

'A new guest at the lodge,' Seth said smoothly. 'Tascha Dennis, Hans Kluyper.'

Hans's living quarters were spotlessly clean and rather fussily over-decorated, little frilly curtains and crocheted

mats nudging rifle racks and tobacco tins. The wall beside
his bed was plastered with luscious pin-ups, all generously endowed. Hans busied himself in the kitchen,
talking non-stop; apparently he averaged one set of visi-
tors a week and in between entertained himself with
books and a shortwave radio, conditions under which
Tascha was certain she also would talk compulsively. She
put in an occasional question and was rewarded with
Hans's life story, discovering he had come here from
Holland twenty-five years ago. So he would have known
Neil Curtis, she thought with a quickening of interest.
If the man Belov had arrived here twenty years ago, Hans
would have known that, too.

Trying not to flinch at the bitterness of Hans's coffee,
she accepted a large piece of bakeapple pie; the fruit was
that of the white-flowered plants she had seen by the
stream, and the conversation left the past in favour of
the flora and fauna of the mine site. Then Seth went to
the jeep to get some supplies he had bought for Hans
in Whitehorse, and to bring in his mail. Tascha seized
her opportunity. She leaned forward intently. 'Hans,
have you ever heard of a man called Belov? He would
have arrived twenty years ago with Neil Curtis.'

Hans had been smiling at her as jovially as any Santa
Claus. But her question wiped the smile from his face.
He said stiffly, almost by rote, 'I know of no one called
that name.'

'Twenty years ago, Hans...try and remember,' Tascha
cried, her ears straining for Seth's return.

'He does not come here ever,' Hans said, and with
daunting formality passed her a plate of molasses
cookies.

Frustrated, for his manner did not ring true, Tascha
took a cookie she did not want and heard Seth at the
door of the shack. Instantly, Hans was all joviality again,
exclaiming over the supplies and scrutinising his two

letters, turning them over and over in his hands but not yet opening them. Tascha went to stand by the window, oppressed by the limitations of Hans's life as much as by his faulty memory. A white seagull was perched on the roof of one of the other buildings.

'A mew gull,' Hans called cheerfully. 'Feed him a cookie, if you like, he is very tame.'

Glad to get out of the claustrophobic little room, Tascha took a molasses cookie from the plate and went outside. The gull, yellow-eyed and wary, did not seem particularly tame to her. When she crouched down, throwing pieces of the cookie on the gravel, the gull flapped ponderously to the ground, fifteen feet from the nearest piece. Tascha backed away, close to Hans's shack, to give the bird more space. It eyed her suspiciously. She retreated further, until she was right under the window. The gull grabbed a chunk of cookie, gulping it uncouthly, and over her head Tascha heard Hans say, 'Seth, your pretty little friend, she asked about Belov.'

'Like hell she did!'

'*Ja, ja,* as soon as you go outside. It is OK, I tell her nothing.'

Tascha had heard enough. Bent low, she moved away from the shack as stealthily as she could in Seth's boots. The gull took to the air with an outraged squawk. Tascha tossed it the last of the crumbs, as if nothing else was on her mind, and strolled back towards the shack. All her doubts had vanished. Hans knew about Belov; and Seth knew of his whereabouts. She would swear to those two facts in any court of the land.

Seth opened the door of the shack. 'Ready to go?' he said to Tascha.

He was a man of subtlety; he had neither raised his voice nor frowned at her. But she could feel like a cold wind his displeasure, and with a pang of premonition wondered if the discovery of Belov would automatically

lose her Seth's friendship. High cost, she thought unhappily. Would the mysterious Belov be worth such a
loss? She had no way of knowing.

All this had flashed through her mind in a second.
'Let me say goodbye to Hans,' she replied.

Although Hans kissed her on both cheeks, he did it
dutifully rather than with enthusiasm. Nor did he
propose, Tascha noticed wryly. She waved goodbye as
the jeep drove down the track. The mew gull wailed a
mournful complaint. 'What a lonely life Hans leads,'
she murmured.

'It suits him,' Seth said brusquely, and for the next
hour that was the sum total of their conversation.

The blue and white sign at the border of the Northwest
Territories said with rather charming brevity:

'Welcome to Northwest Territories
WARNING: Proceed at your own risk
The road is not maintained
and bridges are not safe'

Very soon Tascha realised the sign had not overstated
the dangers. The road degenerated into a double track,
with weeds in the centre, fireweed hedging it in. They
came to a wide river, where the water riffled over the
rocks and the thick timbers of the bridge had collapsed
on themselves, lying half in and half out of the water
like a tired old animal that could not take another step.
As Seth forged the river, Tascha began to understand
the logic of Eddie's packhorses. Then she forgot about
Eddie, concentrating solely on keeping her seat as the
jeep lurched into gullies, heaved itself over boulders,
bumped through creek beds, and straddled washouts.
Through all this, Seth drove with care, concentration
and extreme competence; and in silence.

Then the road improved minimally as they drove the length of a widespread valley, the green lowlands patterned by cloud shadows and silver lakes, the mountains snow-patched. Tascha looked around her in wonder. 'I've never seen a more beautiful place!' she said spontaneously. 'Seth, would you stop for a minute so I can get out?'

He gave her an unreadable glance, but stopped the jeep. She carefully slid to the ground and limped ahead of the jeep, then swept the valley with her gaze and felt again an exhilarating sense of adventure. She was with a man who fascinated her; and she was drawn to this land by the certainty that she was going to meet her own destiny. She felt as alert as the wolf and as free as the eagle. She felt wonderful.

She turned back to the jeep and climbed in, her eyes shining and her cheeks flushed. 'If you'd taken me back to Twin Peaks, I would never have seen this!' she exclaimed. 'There's so much space... I feel as though I'm expanding to fit it.'

'A typical delusion in the north,' Seth said repressively.

Tascha said boldly, 'You really don't want me here, do you?'

'No, I don't.'

'I don't see how you can be so petty in the midst of all this beauty!' she cried, gesturing with her hand to indicate the valley.

'Pettiness is hardly an accurate word for my state of mind,' Seth said tightly. 'Now, will you please be quiet so I can concentrate on keeping us out of the ditch?'

'I trust you're not as rude to all the other guests,' she retorted.

'I've already told you the lodge is booked—so I'm not considering you as a guest. An interloper, more likely. Be quiet, Tascha.'

She obeyed, her mouth a thin line. If she had deceived him, he was equally guilty of deceit; however, she preferred to keep to herself her certainty that Belov was somewhere in the vicinity of the lodge. She had few enough advantages in this cat-and-mouse struggle between her and Seth. She had to hold on to the ones she had!

CHAPTER FIVE

AN HOUR later, Seth stopped the jeep at the top of a slight rise. Ahead of them a vast area of treeless tundra was rimmed by a circle of mountains. Ponds glittered like shards of glass. Then movement caught Tascha's eye, and she saw two animals ambling along a ridge, occasionally stopping to graze.

'Caribou,' said Seth. 'The lodge is up there.'

The small cluster of buildings on top of a low hill commanded a view of the whole plain. 'How you must love it here!' Tascha breathed, clasping her hands in childlike pleasure.

'I didn't stop for you to admire the view,' he said in a clipped voice. 'There are a few things I want to make clear before you arrive at the lodge.'

She dragged her eyes away from the hill, feeling her nerves tighten with apprehension. 'Yes?'

'I told you I was booked up. I've had to turn several potential guests away, among them some relatives of people who are here now, the Bryants. So obviously you can't be seen as a guest. Besides, all the cabins are full. You'll sleep in a tent and you'll work in the kitchen while you're here—Mae could do with some help. Do you understand?'

In one stroke, Seth was keeping her occupied and away from the guests, so she would not have the opportunity to search for Belov. 'Yes,' she said evenly, 'I understand very well.'

But he was not finished with her. Raw hostility in his face, he said, 'In Whitehorse, when we bumped into each

73

other in the hotel corridor, you knew that you were coming here, didn't you?'

It was a question she could have anticipated. She raised her chin. 'Yes,' she said, and let the single word hang in the air without apology or explanation.

'Did you enjoy making a fool out of me?'

Her eyes fell. 'No,' she said. 'I hated it.'

'Oh, sure,' he said disagreeably. 'Come off it—you must have had a good laugh, Tascha.'

'No, Seth, I didn't laugh at you,' she rejoined, her eyes fierce with honesty.

He took her by the chin. 'Have you ever thought of going in for the stage?'

His face was so close, she could see tiny flecks in his eyes, like splinters of gold in the blackness of stone. 'Seth,' she said, 'I'll sleep in the tent and I'll cook for you. But I won't put up with being insulted by you.'

If anything, he looked even more hostile. 'Oh? How do you propose to stop me?' he grated, then bent his head and kissed her hard on the mouth.

It was a kiss intended as punishment, as a display of power and superior strength. Tascha wrenched her head free and scrambled across the seat as far from him as she could, glaring at him through a sheen of tears. 'Don't!' she choked. 'That's a horrible thing to do!'

Savagely he wiped his mouth with the back of his hand. 'Then don't make a fool of me again,' he said, and threw the jeep in gear.

Tascha stared fixedly out of the window. By the time the jeep had bumped up the long, curving driveway to the lodge, she had herself under control. Seth said briefly, 'I'll show you your tent and then I'll take you to meet Mae. The guests are out hiking with Martin, he's my helper.'

The lodge, paradoxically, looked as warm and welcoming as it had in the brochure. Seth marched her past three of the cabins, then across a little gully and down a slope to a white canvas tent and another cabin that stood apart from the rest of the buildings. Tascha knew instinctively that the cabin was Seth's.

The tent had a raised wooden floor, a metal cot, a tiny table and a kerosene lamp. All the comforts of home, thought Tascha, and dumped her bedroll on the cot and her canvas bag on the floor. Then she went back outside. The open tent flaps looked out over the tundra and the distant mountains; on a grassy mound just down the slope, a small brown animal popped out of a hole, gave Tascha an affronted look, squawked twice in a nasal voice, and vanished as quickly as it had appeared. She gave an incredulous laugh. 'What was that?'

'Arctic ground squirrel. Their burrows are all around the lodge. The Inuit and Indians call them sik-siks because of the noise they make.'

Two smaller squirrels shot out of a tunnel and chased each other madly around the burrow, rolling and tumbling on the ground, shaking some low-growing pink flowers like a miniature windstorm. As Tascha laughed again in sheer delight, Seth said with exaggerated forbearance, 'Tascha, dinner has to be cooked by six-thirty.'

Unable to summon up any anger, she grinned at him. 'Yes, boss.'

He said abruptly, 'Your eyes are a deeper blue than the sky.'

She could feel herself blushing. She said hurriedly, 'And my face must be redder than those flowers, whatever they are.'

'Willow-herb. Same genus as fireweed.'

'You know a lot about the north, don't you?'

'I've been coming here since I was a kid.'

She said tentatively, 'You must miss your father here.'

Seth looked back towards the lodge, his profile clearly etched against the sky. 'I sometimes still expect him to walk out between the buildings...'

'And your mother?' Tascha asked quietly.

'My mother died years ago, when I was twelve.'

'Your father never remarried?'

Seth's face closed. 'No.'

A forbidden subject, obviously, she thought with a pang of compassion. She said, 'Let's go and meet Mae. I worked one summer as a short-order cook, so I'll have you know you're getting experienced help.'

There was a small silence before Seth said, 'I have trouble seeing you as a cook.' And she knew that was not what he had planned to say.

She answered, with insouciance, 'When the rent man's at the door, you'd be surprised by what you'll do.'

But Seth's face was very serious. 'You haven't had an easy life, have you, Tascha?'

Pleased by his interest, she admitted, 'My career has been what you might call chequered. I've also been a waitress, a barmaid, and a scholarship student in English literature.'

He stepped closer to her, resting one hand on her shoulder, his eyes baffled. 'Tascha, I——'

She waited, feeling agonisingly close to him, desperately wanting their intimacy to continue. But then his hand fell to his side. He said roughly, 'I don't know what in hell's wrong with me. Come on.'

She tramped behind him in the heavy boots, noticing again how his black hair curled on to his nape, wanting to run her fingers up the tanned, corded neck and bury them in his hair, gaining an inkling for the first time in her life of the power of sexual attraction. Until she had met Seth, she had never wanted a man, she realised that now. She had been as unawakened as any princess in the tower. But she wanted Seth. And, unless she was very much mistaken, he wanted her. Against his will, maybe. But he still wanted her.

He had led her to the back door of the lodge. Opening the door, he ushered her inside. 'I've brought you a helper, Mae,' he said. 'This is Tascha Dennis. She's marooned here until Sunday and can't afford to pay, so I'm putting her to work.'

It was a masterly mis-statement of the events of the past three days. Tascha smiled cordially and held out her hand. 'Hello, Mae.'

Mae was grey-haired and motherly, her comfortable bulk wrapped in a big red apron. 'Pleased to meet you,' she said.

Tascha took off her boots and left them neatly by the door. 'What would you like me to do first?'

Mae looked her over, nodded as if satisfied and said, 'Well, now, you can start peeling some potatoes, and then I'll show you round the kitchen. I like to have dinner on time, they're always hungry after hiking all day.' She flapped her hands at Seth. 'Away you go—we've got work to do.' And Seth left without a murmur.

Realising she was being indiscreet, but unable to help herself, Tascha said, 'You certainly know how to handle him!'

'Known him since he was a little un,' Mae said companionably. 'Tried to be a bit of a mother to him, but of course no one could take her place. Not with him or with his daddy.' She sighed pensively. 'Well, I mustn't stand here gossiping. The potatoes are in the big cupboard and all the knives are in that drawer.'

So Mae, like Hans, had been associated with the Curtis family for years, Tascha thought, picking potatoes out of the brown sack and knowing that she must ask Mae about Belov. Not today, in case Mae reacted as Hans had. But soon, because time was short.

The kitchen was modern, well organised and very clean. After the potatoes were peeled, Tascha was relegated to make a spinach salad from fresh spinach grown in plastic frames outside, a piece of horticultural ingenuity she had to admire. She and Mae worked well together, Mae keeping a sharp eye on her but not smothering her with too many directions. By the time the guests started to filter into the spacious panelled dining-room, which was joined to the kitchen by two hatches, the huge hip of beef was carved, the gravy was bubbling on the stove and the vegetables were drained.

The guests helped themselves, buffet-style, and Mae calmly introduced Tascha to each one of them. Preoccupied with keeping the bowls filled with vegetables, Tascha smiled and nodded, knowing she would not remember a quarter of their names. Two she would remember, though. Jasmine Bryant, who at fifteen or sixteen was dressed like a thirty-year-old vamp in a New York bar, and her father Clyde, for whom the only appropriate word was 'nice': a rather dull brown sparrow who had hatched a gaudy parrot, thought Tascha. Seth was late arriving for dinner. Jasmine, who had saved a seat at her table, immediately called him over, her mascaraed lashes working overtime, her cleavage tilted in his direction. Tascha turned away to replenish the gravy.

When the guests were relaxing at their tables with coffee, Tascha and Mae helped themselves to food and ate perched at the counter. Unfortunately, this gave Tascha an uninterrupted view of Jasmine's activities. She would have liked to dismiss the girl as a ludicrously overdressed teenager who had—naturally enough—an innocent crush on Seth; but quantities of make-up could not disguise the beauty of Jasmine's face with its wide green eyes and tumbled red curls, and her inappropriate clothes merely emphasised her lithe, exquisite figure. She exuded raw sex, thought Tascha glumly, chewing her carrots.

What man could withstand those pouting lips and perfect, upthrust breasts?

Apparently Seth could. Before Jasmine had finished her coffee, he pushed back his chair and excused himself, crossing the room to enter the kitchen. 'Excellent meal,' he said, smiling affectionately at Mae, whose red apron overflowed her chair. 'You make the best spinach salad I've ever eaten.'

Mae winked at Tascha. 'Well now, Tascha made the salad,' she said. 'She's a fine helper, Seth—you should persuade her to stay the rest of the summer.'

His smile froze. 'She has to go back on Sunday,' he said, then turned to Tascha, adding formally, 'Once you're through in here, feel free to join the others in the lounge. We have telescopes set up so you can see the caribou, and you might spot a grizzly—a young male's been hanging around the last couple of weeks.'

'Join the guests there?' Tascha asked clumsily.

'This isn't your average hotel, Tascha,' he replied. 'Once you're off duty, you're free to mingle with the guests. All the staff are. We've always run the lodge that way.'

So she had been overly suspicious to think he was trying to isolate her from the other people at the lodge. 'I'd love to get a closer look at a caribou.'

'Shouldn't be any problem, there are always groups of them browsing out there.' He gave her an unexpected smile. 'You've got gravy on your chin,' he said, and left the kitchen.

'Well now,' said Mae, whose bright little eyes missed very little, 'first time he's ever praised the spinach salad.' She heaved herself down from the stool. 'No dish-washers here, dear, I'm afraid. Except for us.'

By moving quickly and efficiently Tascha did more than her share of the cleaning up, for Mae was not a young woman and her face was flushed from the heat.

When the kitchen was restored to order, Mae firmly dismissed her. 'Six-thirty in the morning comes early,' she said. 'Seth will wake you, I expect.'

Tascha escaped from those all-too-observant eyes and went to the tent. It would be hers for the next four nights. Determined not to worry about how quickly that time might pass, she did her best to turn the tent into a home, neatly making the bed, putting her books on the table and her sneakers on the floor. There was nowhere to hang her clothes, so after changing into a pink sweater she placed her bag against the wall of the tent. She then brushed her hair into a loose knot on the top of her head, put on some lipstick and perfume, and would vehemently have denied that these activities had anything to do with Jasmine.

The lounge was on the second storey at one end of the main lodge and had plate-glass windows on three sides, so that when Tascha stood in the middle of the room she felt surrounded by the mountains and the sky. Various of the guests chatted to her in a friendly way, and Martin Read, Seth's bearded, fifty-year-old helper, who was a biology professor in Toronto in the winter, showed her how to work the telescopes and focus on the caribou. Fascinated, she watched a group of four cows and two calves browse their way along a ridge, every now and then raising their blunt-nosed, chocolate-brown heads to test the air.

Relinquishing the telescope to someone else, she gravitated to the bookshelves, well stocked with books on wildlife and a wide range of novels. A wood stove took up one corner of the room and a bar another, while assorted comfortable chairs and cushions encouraged relaxation. Tascha took out a book on caribou and began to read. She was acutely conscious of being happy. Destiny or no, this place felt like home.

When Seth came up the steps an hour later she gave him an uncomplicated smile of pleasure, for in the interim Martin had pointed out a gyrfalcon and a bull caribou. She was sitting on the floor on a cushion, the book spread in her lap; her sweater subtly emphasised the swell of her breasts and the slender line of her throat. But then her smile faded, because Jasmine came bounding up the stairs behind Seth, wearing a pair of jeans so tight Tascha wondered she could move at all, and the same low-necked sweater. Or would you call it high-waisted? thought Tascha nastily, burying her head in the book.

However, the lounge's atmosphere of serenity seemed to subdue even Jasmine, who contented herself with hanging on to Seth's every word and, more literally, to his arm. She all too frequently brushed her breasts against his sleeve and her hip against his thigh, and ran her tongue over her lips every time he glanced her way, until Tascha wanted to scream at her or throw the scholarly tome on *Rangifer tarandus* at the two of them.

This was hardly fair of her, for Seth was doing nothing to encourage Jasmine and indeed moved away from her at every chance he got. He keyed out a flower specimen for elderly Mrs Bosley, found an article on marmots for Mr Bosley and then moved to one of the telescopes. A few minutes later he said, 'Tascha, do you want to see a grizzly?'

Jasmine cried, 'Oh, show me!'

'Tascha first—she hasn't seen one yet.'

Tascha crossed the room, trying to ignore the truly malevolent look Jasmine gave her. Seth's arm went around her shoulders and he guided her hand to the focus knob. 'See it?'

A large, dark brown bear sprang into view, shambling across the circular field of the telescope, so close Tascha felt she could reach out and touch its massive shoulders, from which dangled long hanks of moulting fur. The bear stopped to sniff at a bush, its head swinging from side to side.

When Tascha looked up her face was alight with wonder. 'He walks as if he owns the place,' she said.

Seth's arm still seemed to be around her shoulders; he gave her a little squeeze. 'The eagle rules the sky and the grizzly the tundra.'

Then Jasmine rudely elbowed Tascha aside, saying, 'Let me see,' and Seth had to release Tascha. She went back to her cushion, warmed by the memory of his smile and not minding Jasmine's tactics nearly as much.

Clyde Bryant came to sit beside her as Tascha was reading about gyrfalcons. He showed her photos of some of the birds she might expect to see in the vicinity of the lodge, his voice alive with enthusiasm of the avid bird-watcher, and she warmed to his friendliness and good manners, wishing some of the latter could rub off on his daughter.

Seth left the lounge, Jasmine on his heels, and gradually it grew too dark to read. The ponds turned to opal, the sky awash with pink and palest orange, the mountains purple-hued. Tascha stood at the window and watched in silence, feeling a peace such as she had rarely known in the rough-and-tumble years of her upbringing. Olga seemed long-dead and Belov of little importance. She was Tascha. Complete within herself.

When the sun had disappeared behind the mountains, she left the lounge and walked to her tent. Yellow light spilled from the windows of Seth's cabin. Quelling the mad urge to open the door and put her arms around him, she stooped under the tent flaps and got ready for bed.

Tascha woke at six the next morning. For a few minutes she lay snuggled in her sleeping-bag, relishing its warmth and softness. But the sun was streaming against the roof of the tent and she wanted to see the tundra in the light of morning. She scrambled out of the down bag and pulled on her clothes. Last night she had rather cleverly left a container of water by her tent to wash her face and brush her teeth; the cold water drove any vestiges of sleep from her brain, as did the lingering soreness in her knees and heels. Putting on Seth's boots, she walked down the hill past the sik-sik burrow.

The air smelled cool and fresh; the ponds were now pale gold, the sky a soft blue. As she sat down on a rock, drinking it all in, from further down the slope a bird whistled plaintively, 'Chu-wheat...chu-wheat'. In its cry was all the mystery and loneliness of the tundra. She hugged her knees, and again was aware of happiness.

That Seth should speak behind her seemed an extension of that happiness. 'Do you hear the plover?' he said softly.

'It's beautiful.'

'I went to wake you, but you'd gone.' He reached out a hand. 'Come with me, I want to show you something.'

His fingers were warmly curled around her own, and she knew with a strange sense of predestination that she would follow him wherever he led her. Could it be that Seth was the destiny that awaited her here in the mountains? she wondered in confusion. Seth the man who would change her life...not Belov?

Seth led her past another sik-sik burrow to a slope where the ground was covered with tiny blue flowers. He knelt, picked a single flower stalk and held it out to her. She stooped down. 'Alpine forget-me-nots,' he said. 'They're the exact colour of your eyes.' Then he leaned forward to tuck the flowers in her hair and the beauty of his gesture was also a part of the morning.

Tascha could think of nothing to say. But her eyes glowed the deep blue of the tiny flowers and her lips were curved in an unconscious smile. With a sudden exclamation, Seth took her in his arms. Off balance, she fell backwards on to the carpet of forget-me-nots, and as she felt the weight of his body along the length of hers she knew he was going to kiss her and exulted in the fierce intensity of his gaze. He had never kissed her as passionately as he did then, nor had she responded so unabashedly, her lips parted, her hands buried in the thick black hair, her body a surrendering curve. As his hand slid from her shoulder to the rise of her breast, she was pierced by an aching sweetness that she had never experienced before, and was suddenly, primitively, glad that she had never made love with a man before. She wanted Seth to be the first.

His hand was still at her breast, bringing her so much pleasure that she moaned deep in her throat. He raised his head, his eyes searching her face, and with his fingertip traced the brush of her lashes on her cheek. 'I've just discovered a new variety of forget-me-not,' he said huskily. 'A truly beautiful blue . . . like sunlit water.'

Tascha gazed up at him in silence, wondering who he was, this black-haired man whose body was pressing hers into the ground. How did he bring her such happiness, such unexpected desire? Were these emotions what the poets called love? She did not know, for love had been all too rare in her twenty-two years, and she had little with which to compare her feelings. She reached up her hand and stroked the line of his cheek. Seth turned his head and kissed her fingers one by one, and as he did so the cry of the plover echoed across the barrens.

Then the spell was broken, for Seth had glanced at the watch on her wrist. 'My God, it's twenty to seven!' he exclaimed. 'We've got work to do.'

He pulled her to her feet. She grabbed at his shirtfront for balance, some of the enchantment of their embrace still lingering in her face. She said with comical dismay, 'You mean I've got to think about pancakes and coffee?'

'And I've got to change a tyre on the bus.' The second vehicle at the lodge was a fourteen-passenger yellow bus.

'I'll probably fry the coffee and boil the pancakes.'

'Mae will keep you in line.'

Somehow these remarks bridged the gap between magic and reality. They began walking towards the lodge, not touching, and when they reached the shed where the vehicles were kept Seth gave her a casual salute and left her. Tascha tried to wipe the smile off her lips before she faced Mae, and pushed open the kitchen door.

Breakfast involved considerably more than pancakes and coffee. Tascha prepared a big bowl of fresh fruit salad, adding raisins and coconut to it; she baked muffins and fried bacon and stirred oatmeal. The guests made astonishing inroads into all this food. Afterwards, she and Mae cleared the table and spread out the ingredients for lunch, so that all the people who were hiking for the day could pack their own. Only then could Tascha herself get breakfast. She buttered a muffin and poured a mug of coffee, deciding that she was very definitely earning her keep at Caribou Lodge.

It was nearly noon by the time the dishes were cleared away and blueberry cheesecake prepared for dessert that evening; Tascha did not have to be back in the kitchen until four. She wandered upstairs to the lounge, which was deserted, and scanned the tundra with the telescopes, finding one lone caribou in the foothills to the west and the party of hikers heading towards a lake to the east; they were too far away to distinguish individuals, although she would be willing to bet that the figure lagging well to the rear was Clyde Bryant, scrutinising everything in feathers.

Footsteps came up the stairs. Jasmine said sulkily, 'Oh, it's you.'

She was wearing a scarlet sweater and the same impossibly tight jeans. Said Tascha non-committally, 'Who were you expecting?'

Jasmine plunked herself into the nearest chair with none of the grace she would have exhibited had Tascha been male. 'Seth,' she pouted.

'He's gone on the hike, hasn't he?' Tascha asked; she had seen him packing a large bundle of sandwiches.

'No. He didn't go. That's why I stayed behind, because I figured I'd be able to spend the day with him.' Jasmine glowered at the distant mountains. 'And now I can't find him.'

Tascha could have made some flip remark or tried to tease Jasmine; but Jasmine's lower lip, heavily outlined in scarlet, was quivering, and the big green eyes were miserable with all the intensity of youth. 'Surely he's somewhere around,' Tascha said gently. 'Perhaps he's working on the jeep.'

'That's one of the first places I looked,' Jasmine said rudely. 'He's not anywhere around—after all, where can you hide in this God-awful place?' She swept the tundra with a venomous lack of appreciation. 'The jeep's gone since this morning. So I bet he took off somewhere on his own.'

Warning bells sounded in Tascha's brain. Seth was not with the rest of the hikers, and the jeep was gone. Belov. Seth had gone to see Belov.

Jasmine's lip was quivering again. 'I don't see why he couldn't have taken me,' she wailed.

If Tascha was correct, she understood very well why Seth had not taken Jasmine. She said soothingly, 'Maybe he's gone to look for grizzlies or wolverines, and he didn't want to expose you to any danger.'

'I'd love to be somewhere dangerous with him,' Jasmine complained. 'Then he could rescue me.'

That Tascha, in a more adult way, would also have gone anywhere with Seth was not much help in dealing with Jasmine. 'I'm sure he'll be back for dinner,' she offered.

'But then everybody else will be here.' Jasmine scowled. 'He's crazy about me, I know that—but he has to be careful when all the other guests are around. That's why I'd hoped we'd have a day to ourselves.' She lifted the shining weight of her red hair in both hands, a gesture which outlined the perfection of her breasts, and said confidingly, 'I'd planned to seduce him today, you see; that's why I'm so upset.'

Tascha blinked, not sure whether to be amused or angry, and said weakly, 'Oh?'

'Mmm...he's so gorgeous, isn't he? That smile of his...and those muscles.' Jasmine rolled her eyes. 'Just to get near him makes me weak at the knees!'

'Jasmine, I scarcely think——'

'Oh, well, Dad and I are staying another week. This is the first time Dad's brought me here, and I nearly died when I heard we were going to be stuck in the middle of nowhere for three whole weeks. But that was before I met Seth.' She let her hair fall to her shoulders, twirling a strand around her fingers; her nails were also scarlet. 'I think I'll go to his cabin one night,' she said dreamily. 'Just walk in the door in my nightdress.' She glanced over at Tascha. 'You know, I was kind of worried when you arrived, figured maybe you were Seth's girlfriend or something. That really would have fouled things up. Although I've got one thing to offer Seth that you haven't—I'm still a virgin, you see.'

Tascha sat up straight. 'What makes you think I'm not?'

Jasmine laughed. 'Come off it—you're too old! I don't know anyone ever eighteen who's still a virgin. All the girls in my school are *determined* not to be. *I'm* going to lose mine with Seth. I've made up my mind to that.'

'He might have something to say on the subject.'

'You haven't seen my nightdress,' Jasmine said complacently. 'He won't be able to resist me . . . just wait 'til I show the girls at school his photo.'

Tascha shook her head, trying to rid herself of the image of Jasmine in Seth's arms, knowing that among her tangled emotions jealousy was definitely a part. Trying to speak objectively, she said, 'Jasmine, Seth isn't a trophy to be gathered. He's a man, with feelings—and you're talking about making love. Not just a physical act that you can boast about to the girls back home.'

Jasmine said scornfully, 'You sound like my father— you're really not with it at all, are you? We're a younger generation, and what we want, we take.'

Tascha got up and went to stand by the window, her shoulders hunched. Surely Seth would not fall into Jasmine's arms, no matter how provocative the nightdress . . . surely? Behind her, Jasmine said with cruel insight, 'Say, I think maybe you're a little bit in love with him yourself.'

'Of course I'm not,' Tascha said in a low voice. 'I just dislike the way you're treating sex as a parlour game.'

'Yeah?' Jasmine drawled. 'Of course, I could hardly blame you for being in love with Seth, who could resist him? But don't get in my way, will you?' She gave a breathless little laugh. 'You're leaving on Sunday, anyway—so the field'll be clear.'

Tascha turned around. 'Jasmine, life isn't so simple that you can always take what you want.'

'Sure it is—you'll see.' Jasmine carelessly waved a hand at her. 'I'm going to go do my nails.'

Tascha stayed where she was, trying to rid herself of an oppressive sense of foreboding. She, Tascha, had never made love to a man. Had never been in love. So what did she know of love that she should talk so confidently to Jasmine? Nothing. She knew nothing about it at all.

As clearly as if Olga was standing in front of her, Tascha could see her scraped-back hair and aquiline nose, her cold, unforgiving eyes. Olga had never loved her, had never given her approval or security or warmth. So Tascha had sought them elsewhere. She had loved school from the beginning, for books opened a whole new world to her, where she could forget the poverty of her home. She excelled in school; worse, in the eyes of her peers, she enjoyed school. So she was always considered something of an oddity, an outsider, even when her beauty blossomed; for her beauty was laced with intelligence and a passionate concern with matters other than school sports and rock idols. She knew she did not fit in school and was sorry, but she could not have altered her nature. Matters did not measurably improve when she was awarded scholarships to university, for the libraries were bigger at the university and she could lose herself all the more easily. A few of the professors recognised her vibrant love of learning, and they became her friends. She sometimes dated other scholarship students, but she had little money for entertainment and no desire to fall in love, so that nothing ever came of these dates.

And then, she thought, she had met Seth, and he, simply by being himself, had roused emotions in her she had scarcely known existed. Desire and its ugly counterpart, jealousy. Happiness and anger. And fear, fear that after Sunday she would never see him again...

Where was he now? If Belov lived near the lodge, it was logical that Seth would visit him, particularly after Seth had been away for a few days. He would not want Tascha—or anyone else—following him. So he had left while she was busy in the kitchen; and she would be willing to bet he would return just before dinner. The kitchen faced the back of the lodge; she would not have a hope of even seeing the direction from which he came.

But she was wrong in this. She was putting cutlery and serviettes on the tables in the dining-room when she saw through the window the black jeep driving back to the lodge from the east, the direction in which the road soon became impassable. She felt a stirring of excitement. If she went down that road and looked for trails leading from it, she might find the man she sought.

Not stopping to think, she hurried into the kitchen. 'Mae, have you ever heard of someone called Belov?' she asked. 'It's possible he's a writer. I think he lives somewhere near here.'

With a great clatter, Mae dropped the spoon she was holding. Tascha quickly stooped to pick it up. 'Well, now, I don't ever recall hearing that name,' Mae said ponderously, looking at the spoon rather than Tascha.

Mae was not an accomplished liar. Tascha said urgently, 'It's terribly important, Mae—I'm not just asking out of idle curiosity. I have to meet him, and I only have until Sunday. I think Seth has been to see him today.'

Mae's brow cleared. 'Well then, you ask Seth, dear. That's your best bet.'

'But Seth won't tell me!'

'He must have his reasons,' Mae said vaguely. 'Ah, there's the salt—I think we should add a little more to the stew, don't you?'

Tascha's fists were clenched in frustration. She released them, feeling as though they belonged to someone else, and picked up a pile of side plates for the tables. When Seth came in the back door a few minutes before dinner, she looked at him unsmilingly. 'Did you have a good day?' she asked.

'Yes, thanks.' He lifted the lid on the pot of stew. 'Smells great. I'm hungry.'

'Were you hiking?'

'You don't have to be hiking to get an appetite up here,' he answered evasively.

'Jasmine was looking for you. She wondered why you didn't take her with you.'

'For all the obvious reasons, Tascha,' he said irritably.

Tascha abandoned caution, Mae's presence forgotten. 'Oh, of course...you didn't want her to know where you were going. Or who you were going to see.'

Seth gripped her by the arm. 'You really do have a vivid imagination, don't you?' he said unpleasantly.

'I have eyes, Seth. And I have ears.'

His fingers tightened. 'Then perhaps you should learn to mind your own business.'

'But who are you to say what is my business and what is not?' she flashed back.

Mae said, very calmly, 'Mr and Mrs Bosley have just entered the dining-room.'

Seth swore under his breath. Letting go of Tascha's arm, he said roughly, 'I'm going to clean up.'

Tascha stared after him. He was wearing well worn leather boots, soft cords tucked into wool socks and a down waistcoat over a chamois shirt: hiking clothes. She had been a fool to challenge him, she thought, angry with herself. If indeed he had visited Belov today, he would make a point of not doing so again until next week, when she was gone. He would not risk revealing Belov's hiding place, not at this juncture.

She took the dinner plates from the warming oven, her mind racing. If she worked very hard tomorrow morning she could be free by eleven. That would give her five hours to hike east along the road, searching for a trail. She must not give up, not when every instinct she possessed told her she was close to her quarry.

CHAPTER SIX

As TASCHA left the kitchen that evening, Clyde Bryant waved to her from the hill behind the lodge. He was carrying binoculars. Tascha was not in the mood for his obsessive enthusiasm for anything with wings; but neither was she in the mood to spend the evening in her tent alone, or in the lounge watching Jasmine twine herself around Seth. She tightened the laces of the pair of old sneakers that Mae had loaned her, that were large enough not to aggravate her blisters, and plodded up the hill.

Her feet crunched in the lichen and dried heather. The tundra, that from a distance could look brown and lifeless, at closer view was sprinkled with the tiny flowers of the north: creamy mountain avens, bright pink moss campion, yellow Arnica like miniature sunflowers, and the turquoise, tightly shut gentians. Trying not to step on any of them, Tascha finally reached Clyde. He passed her the binoculars, getting right down to the essentials.

'On the boulder half-way down the slope there's a long-tailed jaeger.'

Obediently Tascha looked, seeing a sleek grey and white bird rather like a seagull. Behind it, not quite in focus, was the road. The road heading east. She said impulsively, 'Clyde, do you feel like a walk? Or are you tired?'

'Where would you like to go?'

'Along the road away from the lodge.'

'Sure! We pass a couple of ponds, we might see phalaropes and lesser yellowlegs.'

Rather ashamed of herself for taking advantage of his good nature, Tascha trotted along at his side, her eyes peeled for any sign of a track or a side road. Whenever Clyde loaned her the binoculars she would slowly sweep the landscape, searching for a hut, or smoke, or a vehicle. She saw two red-necked phalaropes and was indoctrinated into the mysteries of sandpipers, all of which looked alike to her; she saw caribou, sik-siks, and a flock of longspurs; she saw ducks on a far pond that Clyde assured her were oldsquaws; she saw the brown and white willow ptarmigan. But although they walked for well over an hour along the road she saw no signs of human habitation.

As they turned back, Clyde said with a certain diffidence, 'Jasmine appears to be enjoying herself more than I thought she would.'

Tascha glanced over at him, wondering what possible reply she could make to this his first remark of a personal nature, and marvelling anew that Clyde with his dull brown hair and unmemorable features could have fathered the gorgeous Jasmine. 'That's good,' she said neutrally.

'I'm divorced, you see. Every year I take her on holiday with me. Last year we went to Paris, because I thought she'd like that. But she kept getting lost when she went shopping, and wanting to go into bars...I couldn't keep track of her at all. So this year I brought her here.' He gave Tascha a shy smile. 'I thought she might learn to appreciate nature a little more.'

There was only one aspect of nature that Jasmine was interested in, thought Tascha, smiling back at Clyde.

He went on in a rush, 'She does seem overly interested in boys, if you know what I mean.'

'That's probably natural at her age.'

'I'd like to see her interests a little more balanced.'

So, if the truth were told, would Tascha. 'Have you been divorced for long?' she asked, wanting to leave the subject of Jasmine.

'Quite a long time. Not that I really blame Isabel—my wife. She's the most beautiful woman I've ever seen. The first time I met her I thought she was like a bird of paradise. So I married her. There's really no reason why she should be interested in a dull fellow like me.'

Secretly amused, Tascha said, 'Jasmine must be like her.'

'Yes... Isabel always had an eye for the men, too.' He gave a deep sigh. 'I just hope Jasmine isn't making a nuisance of herself with Seth.'

'I'm sure Seth can look after himself,' Tascha said with perfect truth.

'Very capable fellow. He's a wildlife biologist, you know, teaches at the University of British Columbia. Highly regarded in his field, particularly for his work on grizzlies and caribou.' Clyde gave his dry little laugh. 'And I flatter myself that I've taught him a thing or two about ornithology over the years.'

So the conversation returned to birds and remained there the rest of the way home. But, as they parted at the lodge, Clyde to go to his cabin, Tascha to the kitchen to check all was tidy, Clyde gave her an awkward hug. Plainly impressed by his own daring, he said in a rush, 'Thank you for listening to me talk about Jasmine. I feel as though you understand. Very sweet of you.'

He looked quite overcome. Tascha patted his sleeve and said, 'You're welcome, Clyde. See you tomorrow.'

She watched him wander off to his cabin, his binoculars never still, and smiled to herself. It was just as well Clyde didn't understand Jasmine. He'd be horrified if he did!

The kitchen door opened behind her and Seth's voice said, 'Because I said you could mix with the guests in the lounge, I didn't mean you should become overly familiar with them, Tascha.'

She gave a nervous start and turned around. 'I beg your pardon?' she said frostily.

'You're taking advantage of certain laxity in the rules.'

'Are you insinuating that I'm leading Clyde on?'

'It certainly looked that way to me.'

'That says more about your suspicious nature than about my actions,' she snapped.

'Clyde is the shyest of men—he does not make a habit of hugging strange women!'

Tascha discovered that she was rather pleased by Seth's anger, which quite possibly denoted jealousy; she did not want to be the only one suffering from that unpleasant emotion. She said demurely, 'Only because they don't know how to fly.'

'You have an answer for everything, don't you? Or do you?' Seth suddenly gripped her shoulders and showered half a dozen kisses on her upturned face, ending by kissing her hard on the mouth. 'Do you have an answer for that?' he said sardonically, and headed back towards his room.

She did not. Her breath seemed to be trapped in her throat, while her heart was trying to leap from her body. As Seth disappeared, Tascha said several rude words in French, words Olga would have been justified in frowning upon, and headed for her tent.

When Tascha woke in the morning, her first action was to pack her haversack for the walk east, putting in an extra pair of sneakers, several plasters, and a clean pair of socks. Then she went to the kitchen to start breakfast. She was passing the Bosleys their poached eggs when Seth said in a carrying voice that overrode the normal conversation in the dining-room, 'You must come with us today, Tascha. We're going to hike along the creek to the lake. I'll send Martin ahead with the others and wait for you.'

She gave him an insincere smile. 'I'd rather stay around the lodge today, Seth, thanks.'

Clyde said fussily, 'You must come, Tascha. Time you learned to distinguish one duck from another.'

Mrs Bosley chimed in, 'Do come, dear. The flowers along the creek are so beautiful, and it'll probably be your only chance to see them if you're leaving on Sunday.'

Mr Bosley smoothed his white moustache and added with heavy gallantry, 'We would enjoy your company as much as we enjoy your cooking.'

Seth said smoothly, 'Seems to be unanimous, Tascha.'

It was not exactly unanimous, because Jasmine was glaring at her. Nevertheless, short of being very rude, Tascha knew she was trapped. She gave Seth a look the twin of Jasmine's and said with saccharine sweetness, 'How kind of you to think of me!'

He raised one brow. 'All part of the service,' he said.

She would have liked to crack a plate of eggs over his head. Holding determinedly to her smile, she refilled the jug of juice and brought out more hot muffins.

Seth gave her no chance to elude him, had she planned to try. He was waiting for her when she left the kitchen, wandered along to her tent with her, hitched her haver-sack over his shoulder as soon as she had put her lunch pack inside and escorted her to the jeep, whistling aim-lessly all the while. She was not convinced his actions were at all aimless, for she was almost sure he was fore-stalling any attempt on her part to search for Belov; she should have been angrier with him than she was. But, as had happened so often since she had come to the lodge, thoughts of Belov seemed to slip elusively from her grasp, leaving her with the reality, the excitement, the conflict that was Seth.

```
************************************************************
* You may have already won a lifetime of cash payments *
* totaling up to $1,000,000.00!  Play our Sweepstakes   *
* Game--Here's how it works...                          *
************************************************************
```

Each of the first three tickets has a unique Sweepstakes number
If your Sweepstakes numbers match any of the winning numbers
selected by our computer, you could win the amount shown
under the gold rub-off on that ticket.

Using an eraser, rub off the gold boxes on tickets #1-3 to
reveal how much each ticket could be worth if it is a winning
ticket. You must return the <u>entire</u> card to be eligible. (See
official rules in the back of this book for details.)

At the same time you play your tickets for big cash prizes,
Harlequin also invites you to participate in a special trial of
our Reader Service by accepting one or more FREE book(s) from
Harlequin Presents.® To request your free book(s), just rub off
the gold box on ticket #4 to reveal how many free book(s) you
will receive.

When you receive your free book(s), we hope you'll enjoy them
and want to see more. So unless we hear from you, every month
we'll send you 8 additional Harlequin Presents®novels. Each
book is yours to keep for only $1.99* each--26¢ less per book
than the cover price! There are <u>no</u> additional charges for
shipping and handling and, of course, you may cancel Reader
Service privileges at any time by marking "cancel" on your
shipping statement or returning a shipment of books to us at our
expense. Either way your shipments will stop. You'll receive
no more books; you'll have no further obligation.

PLUS--you get a FREE MYSTERY GIFT!

If you return your game card with <u>all four gold boxes</u> rubbed
off, you will also receive a FREE Mystery Gift. It's your
<u>immediate reward</u> for sampling your free book(s), <u>and</u> it's yours
to keep no matter what you decide.

P.S.

Remember, the first set of one or more book(s) is FREE. So rub
off the gold box on ticket #4 and return the entire sheet of
tickets today!

*Terms and prices subject to change without notice.

"GIVE YOUR HEART" TO HARLEQUIN SWEEPSTAKES

"GIVE YOUR HEART TO HARLEQUIN" SWEEPSTAKES
If this is a winning ticket, it could be worth

1 **$1,000,000.00**

Rub off to reveal potential value if this is a winning ticket: ►

UNIQUE
SWEEPSTAKES
NUMBER: 1B 644336

If this is a winning ticket, it could be worth

2 **$1,000,000.00**

Rub off to reveal potential value if this is a winning ticket: ►

UNIQUE
SWEEPSTAKES
NUMBER: 1C 644078

If this is a winning ticket, it could be worth

3 **$1,000,000.00**

Rub off to reveal potential value if this is a winning ticket: ►

UNIQUE
SWEEPSTAKES
NUMBER: 1D 644059

4 **ONE OR MORE FREE BOOKS**

HOW MANY FREE BOOKS?
Rub off to reveal number of free books you will receive ►

1672765559

Yes! Enter my sweepstakes numbers in the Sweepstakes and let me know if I've won a cash prize. If gold box on ticket #4 is rubbed off, I will also receive one or more Harlequin Presents novels as a FREE tryout of the Reader Service, along with a FREE Mystery Gift as explained on the opposite page. **108 CIH CAN4**

NAME

ADDRESS   APT.

CITY   STATE   ZIP CODE

Offer not valid to current Harlequin Presents subscribers. All orders subject to approval.   PRINTED IN U.S.A.

As the jeep turned left at the bottom of the driveway, heading west, Seth said casually, 'You had plans of your own today, didn't you?'

So he wanted the war in the open. 'I did, yes,' Tascha replied.

Briefly, he took his eyes from the road. 'I wonder what they were.'

She widened her eyes, wondering if they would remind him of forget-me-nots this time. 'You mean you don't know?'

'I could hazard a guess.'

'Go ahead,' she said cordially.

'Why don't you tell me, Tascha?'

'I wouldn't think of spoiling your fun, Seth.' She sighed soulfully. 'It must be wonderful to know everything.'

'I know one thing—the reason you never had a serious boyfriend is because you would have driven the poor guy crazy.'

'Or perhaps I was just more intelligent than he.' There was an unintended bitterness in her words.

'Now, what's behind that remark?'

She grimaced. 'Oh, I always loved school and I always did well at it. But although I was book-smart, I wasn't people-smart—because I never made any secret of the face that I loved school. So, of course, I was never very popular. Kids don't like the ones who are different, who don't go along with the crowd. Hence no serious boyfriend.'

'Hence the scholarships that got you to university,' Seth said shrewdly. 'Because you couldn't have gone otherwise, could you, Tascha?'

'No.'

His face was unexpectedly gentle. 'The money you inherited—will it help you out?'

'At the rate I'm going, it will all be spent,' she said dismissively. 'Are we nearly there?'

'Was it someone close to you who died?' Seth persisted.

'My...mother,' Tascha said, unable to lie to him, but equally unable to share with him all the complicated mixture of emotions that the thought of Olga could conjure up. 'There's the bus parked up ahead,' she added with transparent relief.

'Did she die recently?'

'Three weeks ago. Seth, I don't want to talk about her!'

There was tension in the line of her throat; she was avoiding his gaze. 'I see,' he said thoughtfully, pulling up behind the bus. 'So is her death connected in some way with your search for Belov?'

Tascha stared sightlessly at the hands twisted in her lap. It was, of course. But how could she reveal to anyone else, particularly Seth, the painful dilemma about her parenthood, caused by Belov's letters? Did they represent the chance for a new life? Or was she simply escaping into fantasy? She scarcely knew the answer herself. 'I don't want to talk about her,' she repeated stubbornly.

Had she looked at him, she might have seen compassion in his eyes; but all she heard was the steel of his voice. 'I find it strange that you never use Belov's first name with me—most people do.'

'Most people?'

'Sure. The journalists, the sensation-seekers, the would-be writers...Andrei Belov is the man they're looking for.'

Tascha schooled her face to blankness. 'And which of those categories am I supposed to fit, Seth?'

'Why don't *you* tell me?'

'You started this, Seth—so you finish it!'

He banged his palm against the steering wheel. She gazed at his hand in fascination, remembering how it had rested on her breast, and heard him say, his voice raw with honesty, 'I can't make you fit any of them, Tascha.'

She closed her eyes, letting out her breath in a tiny sigh. 'Thank you,' she whispered.

'I can't make you fit any kind of category. You've deceived me, yet I find myself wanting to trust you. You're not chasing me in any way—not like Jasmine—but I can't keep my hands off you. You're poor, you're beautiful, you're ignorant of the wilderness, you're highly intelligent...' He gave a wry smile. 'And you're a very hard worker. Don't think I'm unaware of how many hours you've put in since you got here.'

She seized the new topic of conversation he had given her with deep relief and looked him straight in the eye. 'Mae's not a young woman—she needs the help.'

'So I am beginning to realise.' He added with a touch of firmness, 'Which does not mean that you'll be staying after Sunday.'

Her lashes flickered, for his words had hurt her, particularly after he had been so honest with her. 'Did it occur to you that I might not want to stay?' she answered with a complete lack of honesty.

Seth turned off the ignition and pocketed the keys. 'It occurred to me that I have very ambivalent feelings on the subject,' he said in a tone of voice that indicated the matter was closed. 'We'll walk up the creek, then cross that ridge. The lake's on the other side.'

Recognising once again Seth's unique ability for knocking her off balance, Tascha slid to the ground.

The creek wound through steep banks lush with tall green grass. The walking was unexpectedly difficult, for the grass concealed hummocks and trenches and sink-holes of thick soupy mud, and, for Tascha at least, the flowers were an added distraction. Their bright faces bobbed around her legs as she and Seth pushed deeper into the meadow. Finally she sat down on a boulder at the stream's edge and said breathlessly, 'I just want to look at everything!'

The water chuckled and gurgled in her ears, the sky reflected the still pools. The colours of the flowers were vivid: red, purple, lavender, yellow and pink. Tascha gave a sigh of contentment. 'Tell me some of their names,' she said.

Seth was studying her rapt face. 'That's another contradiction in you,' he remarked. 'You come from one of the ugliest districts in Montreal, yet you have an unerring eye for beauty.'

She gave her head a little shake. 'I don't want to talk about me. Just tell me the names of the flowers.'

Seth began reeling off words like monkshood, valerian, bluebells, Jacob's ladder and grass-of-parnassus, and all the while he was picking some of the flowers and weaving them into a strand.

'Their names are like poetry,' Tascha murmured.

Seth stepped closer, holding out the finished circlet of flowers. When Tascha saw it she stood up, smiling with delight. 'Oh, Seth, that's beautiful!'

He dropped it over her head. 'I'd like to weave flowers all through your hair,' he said huskily.

As naturally as the flowers lifted their faces to the sunshine, she raised her face for his kiss, a kiss that was as much a part of poetry as the brilliant blossoms and the crystal-clear, dancing water; a quiet poem, serenely beautiful, strangely peaceful, that moved Tascha almost to tears. She looked up at her tall, black-eyed companion in silence, wondering if she would ever understand him, knowing he was as full of paradox as he claimed she was, knowing it was going to tear her heart apart to leave him on Sunday. Still without saying a word, she turned away from him and began walking along the banks of the stream.

When they came to a mossy hummock, thrust up by the ice, they left the creek and angled up the slope towards the ridge. A rain-squall had gathered in the mountains to the north. 'You can watch the weather here,' Seth told her. 'Sunshine, then fifteen minutes of rain, then sun again, often with the most beautiful rainbows. My private name for the creek is Rainbow Creek, because once I saw one arching from south to north, ending in the creek... Have you ever tried to catch the end of a rainbow, Tascha? When I was a kid, I always thought I could.'

Her whole journey seemed like an attempt to catch an elusive, ever-vanishing rainbow. 'Rainbow Creek suits the colours of the flowers,' she said evasively, feeling the breeze from the mountains lift the strands of hair around her face as she trudged towards the ridge. She could not see over the other side to the lake where the guests were gathered; she would have been happy to have gone in the opposite direction and spent the whole day alone with Seth.

She was almost at the crest of the ridge when her ear picked up a sound that was neither her own footsteps nor those of the man behind her. With a primitive tingling of her nerves, she was scanning the ridge just as a massive bull caribou trotted up to the crest from the other side. The caribou saw her in the same instant she saw him. They both stopped in their tracks, the caribou giving a loud snort, its nostrils flared. He was full-grown with a magnificent rack of antlers, his coat glossy, his body alive with energy and a sense of his own power.

For a full ten seconds they stared at each other, the caribou and Tascha. Then, with another snort, the caribou pivoted and in long, springy strides vanished down the ridge.

Tascha found her palms were damp and her heart racing. She stood still, shaken by an encounter so unexpected that it was vividly imprinted in her mind. As Seth came up behind her, she said with deep conviction, 'This is *his* place, isn't it? Not mine. I'm the intruder.'

'Some people never learn that. Never even understand it. They think it's their God-given right to shoot anything up here that moves, so they can hang the trophy on the wall and boast about their exploits to their friends.'

One bullet from a rifle could fell all that power and grace. 'I suppose if I was starving I might be able to shoot a caribou,' Tascha said, feeling her way. 'But not just to hang the antlers on the wall. That would be criminal.'

'I'm glad you see it that way,' Seth said, his eyes warm with approval. 'Look, there's the lake, we'd better join the others.'

The Bosleys wanted to know Tascha's reaction to the flowers, while Clyde was waiting with a telescope all set up to show her oldsquaws, scoters and harlequin ducks. Jasmine took one look at the circle of flowers around Tascha's neck and turned away, her green eyes smouldering. Tascha cursed herself for her thoughtlessness in not tucking the flowers under her jacket, for she had no desire to make an enemy of Jasmine or to hurt her feelings, and tried to concentrate on the flock of anonymous brown blobs on the lake. But nothing could match the encounter with the caribou, and she was almost glad to return to the lodge with Martin at about four o'clock and immerse herself in the straightforward job of cooking dinner.

At dinner time, Seth once again proved his ability to keep her off balance. He announced to all and sundry that they would be hiking east the next day to the creek

where the road became impassable; they would follow
the creek up the mountain to an alpine meadow where
Arctic poppies bloomed. He added casually, 'As it's your
last day, Tascha, you'd better come with us.'

He would be taking her exactly where she wanted to
go! She stared at him in consternation, wondering why
he would flaunt what surely must be the vicinity of
Belov's hiding place. As had happened once before, she
was suddenly paralysed by doubts as to Belov's very
existence. She said in a colourless voice. 'That's
thoughtful of you, Seth,' and picked up a basket of rolls
to replenish it.

She felt tired and oddly depressed that evening, not
in the mood for company. So she curled up on a pile of
cushions in one corner of the lounge and buried her nose
in the book by Andrei Belov. It was not easy reading,
for it was fraught with nuances, mythological references
and symbolism. But his style was exquisite and gradually she was drawn into his world of shadows, where
nothing was as it seemed.

She went to bed early, drawing the tent flaps tightly
shut against the purple-hued mountains; but her sleep
was haunted by phantasmagoria from the book she had
been reading, and she was heavy-eyed the next day.

The hike to the alpine meadows filled Tascha with
mixed emotions. They crossed the creek and scrambled
up a rocky canyon to the long, rounded back of the
mountain, that was like an animal slumbering on its side.
Dark clouds pushed down from the sky. It rained. It
snowed. The sun pierced the clouds, and the arc of a
rainbow spanned the humped grey foothills. But the ends
of the rainbow were hidden from Tascha, and although
she searched in every direction with Clyde's binoculars
she saw no signs of human habitation. She had not
expected to; Seth would not have brought her here had
there been any danger.

She stood a little apart from the others, looking around her. The foothills flowed into each other like earth-bound clouds, their flanks streaked with minerals, the valleys between them a fierce, defiant green; on the mountaintop, the fragile Arctic poppies cupped the capricious sunlight in petals of palest yellow; on a ridge to the west, a small herd of grazing caribou were silhouetted against the sky. Surrounded by beauty, Tascha felt her throat ache with unshed tears, for her presence here was as transitory as the flowers of the poppy; and her relationship with Seth just as transitory. Again she was glad to get back to the lodge, where she threw herself into the preparations for dinner with a frantic energy that made Mae cluck, 'Slow down, dearie, we've got lots of time.'

Tascha had been slicing carrots with vicious accuracy. 'I don't want to leave here, Mae,' she exclaimed, and saw the carrots blur in front of her eyes.

'Ask Seth if you can stay,' Mae said sensibly. 'You're a grand help to me.'

'He says I can't.'

Mae considered Tascha's bent head. 'Don't see why not,' she said. 'Unless he's gone and fallen in love with you.'

Tascha's startled blue eyes met Mae's kindly grey ones. 'If he's fallen in love with me, he'd surely want me to stay?'

'Not Seth.' Mae threw the carrots into a saucepan and settled in for a good gossip. 'I figured out a long time ago that the one thing Seth Curtis is frightened of is love. He can face a grizzly, he can climb mountains, he can put the run on any number of those darned big-game hunters. But he's downright scared of falling in love.' She nodded sagely and added water to the saucepan.

'Why?' Tascha asked baldly.

''Cause of his mother and father. Neil Curtis thought the sun rose and set on his Catherine, and when she died he was like a man groping in eternal darkness. Lost, he was. As useless to himself as he was to anyone else. Certainly not much use to Seth. Seth was only a young boy then, but he was smart enough to put two and two together, and I figure he decided way back then that he was never going to love a woman the way his daddy loved his mother. No, sir. Not worth it.' Mae gave a vigorous nod, plunking the saucepan on the stove. 'There've been any number of young women at the lodge over the years, pretty and nice and bright some of them...but would Seth look at them sideways? Not likely. *He* wasn't going to get involved.'

Tascha felt a painful quickening in her breast. At some level, Seth was certainly involved with *her*. 'I thought he was sending me away because I was looking for Belov,' she said, more to herself than to Mae.

Mae's face closed. 'I wouldn't know about that, dear.' She took a cabbage out of the bottom cupboard and began removing the outer leaves. 'Maybe you're in love with Seth,' she suggested; she was not a devious woman.

'I'm not in love with Seth and he's not in love with me,' Tascha said roundly.

'Well, I don't know...I've seen him watching you times when you didn't know he was. Staring at you the way he stares at a flower he's trying to identify or a bird he's never seen before.' Mae began grating the cabbage. 'Yes, I've seen him do that.'

Not knowing what to say, Tascha said nothing, her mind's eye filled with the image of a small boy whose mother had died and whose father had retreated into a grief-stricken silence. She opened the oven to check on the baked potatoes, wishing she did not feel so unhappy, trying very hard to remember the caribou, the rainbow and the Arctic poppies.

CHAPTER SEVEN

As PART of the routine of the lodge, on Wednesday and Saturday evenings Martin brought in drumloads of water from the nearest creek, heated them for showers, and fired up the sauna. 'We send the guests home clean,' he had told Tascha with a laugh. The guests had their showers in alphabetical order; staff came after that, Seth last of all. The water was still stingingly hot when it was Tascha's turn. She soaped herself all over, shampooed her hair, then stretched out on a towel in the sauna for ten minutes, relaxing her muscles and emptying her mind.

The air struck cold on her face when she went outdoors. Heavy clouds had massed in the sky, and the mountains were already blurred by distant rain. She shivered, scurrying to Martin's cabin to tell him the sauna was empty, then going to the lounge to chat with the guests. Jasmine was conspicuous by her absence, rather to Tascha's relief, because ever since the incident of the necklace of flowers the girl had been less than friendly. She stayed for over an hour, then went back to her tent to get her book. But it was not on her bed or on the little wooden table, and suddenly she remembered she had taken it to the bathhouse with her to read in the sauna. She must have left it there.

She glanced at her watch; Seth would surely be finished by now. Bracing herself against the cold, she ran to the bathhouse. The light was still on. She hesitated on the step before deciding Seth might be in the shower and consequently would not see her. She cupped her hands around her eyes and peered through the steamy glass panels in the door to see if her book was on the bench.

It was. She was reaching for the door-handle when she saw something else: a man's naked form stepping from behind the shower curtain at the far end of the room. Seth. For a moment she was transfixed by his beauty, long-limbed, narrow-flanked, deep of chest. But then another figure moved out of the shadows near the sauna door, a woman, nude, her lissom white body topped by a head of flaming red hair. The woman was Jasmine. She glided over to Seth, and as she put her arms around him the two figures blended into one.

Tascha made a choking sound in her throat, whirled and raced across the rough ground towards her tent, breathing as harshly as she had when she was running from the wolves, and with something of the same panic in her mind. The unimaginable had become real, confronting her with all the demons in hell. She ran as if running for her life!

In her tent, she drew the flaps shut and sat hunched over on her bed. If only she could erase from her brain the image of Jasmine's white body approaching Seth; of the graceful curve of her arm as she had wrapped it around his neck, of the blackness of his hair over the flame-red of hers... So this is jealousy, Tascha thought in horror, this sickness, this anger, this pain. I cannot bear it! I cannot bear to think of him in her arms.

She did bear it, because she had no choice. But she was shivering uncontrollably when she got into bed, and the down folds of her sleeping-bag seemed no protection against a cold that was bone-deep. She would leave here tomorrow and go back to Montreal where she belonged, and she would forget the black-haired man who had woven flowers into a necklace for her and shown her the lonely beauty of the tundra; and she would forget the

other man, the one she had come to find, for he was as
much illusion as Seth.

She must eventually have fallen asleep. It was pitch-
dark when she awoke, struggling out of a terrifying
dream in which she was drowning in the cold waters of
a storm-tossed lake. Scarcely knowing what was real and
what was not, she turned on to her back, hearing rain
lash the walls of the tent and wind snap the canvas flaps
back and forth. She was cold and wet, just as she had
been in the dream.

Trying to understand, she fumbled at her sleeping-bag.
The side against the wall of the tent was soaking wet,
and the rain had seeped into her cotton-knit nightgown,
chilling her to the bone.

Tascha lay still, wondering what she should do,
knowing there were dry clothes in her bag, but no spare
sleeping-bag. Two choices, she thought unhappily. Get
dressed and head for the lodge. Or stay where she was.

She hunched over to the dry side of the down bag.
But the wet part slopped against her back, dampening
more of her nightdress. Acutely miserable, she tried to
rally her sense of humour, or even a sense of ridiculous;
but it was as difficult as trying to light damp firewood.
She was cold. She was wet. And smothering her like the
wet folds of the sleeping-bag was a dreadful loneliness,
her thoughts the black thoughts of the longest part of
the night. Olga had never loved her; the man who had
written those letters twenty years ago knew nothing of
her; Seth could not wait for her to be gone.

She buried her face in the dry side of the pillow,
loathing herself for such flagrant self-pity, but unable
to escape it, listening to the wind tug at the tent flaps
like a thief in the night. Abruptly, unable to bear her
own thoughts, she began struggling with the zipper on
her bag. Freeing herself, she put her bare feet to the floor,
and, bent double, fumbled for her carry-all in the dark.

There were matches in the bag and the stub of a candle on the little table. At least she could banish the darkness.

One side of the carry-all was also wet. With icy fingers, Tascha sorted through her damp jeans and shirts, willing herself not to cry. But the matchbox seemed dry. She opened it carefully and struck a match on the side of the box. The tiny flame flared up. She carried it over to the table and lit the candle, which sputtered, then began to burn a steady, blue-centred flame.

The roof of the tent was sagging inwards, the fabric saturated with moisture, and briefly Tascha was angry that Seth could have put her in a tent that leaked. But she was too uncomfortable to sustain the anger for long, and too miserable. Her jacket, which she had left in the middle of the floor, seemed to be the only dry garment she possessed. She wrapped it around her and sat huddled on the floorboards, trying to get up her courage for the dash to the lodge.

Suddenly the tent flaps were yanked open. Tascha gave an undignified screech. Seth said testily, 'Why in God's name are you sitting on the floor?'

As clearly as if it had just happened, she saw super-imposed over his tanned, naked body Jasmine's white limbs. 'Because it's the only dry place in this god-damned tent,' she yelled. 'Go away!'

He stepped into the tent, stooping low to avoid brushing the roof, then pulling the flaps closed behind him. In the flickering light of the candle, he looked at her bed. 'Tascha, don't you know anything?' he demanded. 'You never put anything against the wall of a canvas tent, because if it rains the water goes straight through. Everyone knows that.'

'Everyone except me.'

'Even your clothes are wet! How long have you been like this? You'll catch pneumonia!'

'As I'm leaving here tomorrow, that need hardly concern you,' Tascha said, slicing off each word as if she were wielding one of Mae's knives. '*You* can leave my tent any time you like.'

Seth's brows drew together in a scowl. 'How the hell can I leave you here like this? You'd better come to my cabin.'

'Congratulations,' she seethed. 'That has to be the most ungracious invitation I have ever received in my whole life. You'll forgive me if I turn it down. After all, I wouldn't want to disturb Jasmine.'

With dangerous quietness, Seth said, 'Now, just what do you mean by that?'

Trying to sound as though she didn't care, but betrayed by an uncontrollable quiver in her voice, Tascha cried, 'Seth, I *saw* you!'

His eyes intent on her face, he said even more quietly, 'What did you see, Tascha?'

'I saw you and Jasmine together.' She jerked her head away from those all-too-discerning black eyes. 'Seth, how could you? She's not even sixteen!'

'Tascha, look at me... please.'

Slowly, she turned her head back, her eyes swimming with tears. All the anger had vanished from Seth's face. He said forcefully, 'I'm assuming that what you saw was me step out of the shower and Jasmine, as naked as a baby, wrap herself around me—right?'

Tascha nodded miserably. Making no attempt to touch her, Seth went on, 'You should have stayed around. You'd have seen Jasmine get dressed quicker than she'd ever gotten her clothes on before, and leave. That's what you would have seen. And believe me, she won't do that again. Not with me, anyway.'

'I didn't stay around,' Tascha said shakily.

His eyes were trained on hers. 'I had no idea she was there—you must believe me, Tascha. I did not instigate that little scene in any way, and I ended it as soon as I realised what was happening.'

'I do believe you.' Tascha buried her face in her hands, conscious of an overwhelming relief and an urge to cry her eyes out. 'I was a fool, Seth—I should have known. She even told me she was planning to seduce you.'

He pulled her hands from her face, then scrupulously released them. 'As the old song says, it takes two to tango. Let me be honest with you at least this far, Tascha—ever since I first saw you, I've wanted you. I don't have to tell you that. I'm not the slightest bit interested in Jasmine or anyone else. How could I be when I'm obsessed with you?'

Although she was not sure she cared for the word 'obsessed', Tascha managed a weak smile. 'Then the last place in the world I should be is in your cabin.'

'Yeah... but I can't leave you here, you're soaked to the skin. Tell you what, we'll go to my cabin, I'll start a fire and lend you some dry clothes, and then I'll go and sleep in the lodge.'

She smiled at him, knowing she had made a fool of herself over the Jasmine incident; although Seth had been as unfailingly polite to Jasmine as he was to all the guests, he had never encouraged her advances in any way. She, Tascha, had known that. But she had allowed jealousy to blind her to Seth's integrity. She shut her mind to all that that jealousy implied and said, 'A fire and some dry clothes sound wonderful.'

She put on her sneakers and pulled the hood of her jacket over her head. Seth backed out of the tent, holding the flap for her. When she stepped down to the ground, the night seized her, the wind whipping her hood back, the rain stinging her face like the jabbing of tiny fingernails. Seth grabbed her hand. 'Come on!' he shouted.

She ran at his side, clutching his hand like a lifeline, and the wild part of her, the part Olga had never been able to subdue, exulted in the wind and the rain. Seth pulled open the cabin door and almost lifted her inside, slamming the door shut behind him. His movements quick and deft, he lit the oil lamp on the table. Tascha sagged against the wall, trying to catch her breath, her blue eyes laughing at him from a drenched face.

Her jacket had fallen open. Her nightdress, because it was wet, clung to her body, to the fullness of hip and the slim curve of waist, to her breasts, rising and falling with her quickened breathing; the nipples were sharp under the thin fabric.

His own breath caught in his throat. He said violently, 'Oh, God, Tascha, I want you so much!' Then, word becoming action, he took her in his arms and kissed her.

But her face was ice-cold and her body clammy. With a sound between a moan and a laugh, Seth raised his head. 'You've got to get out of those clothes,' he said, 'or you *will* catch pneumonia.'

'Catch pneumonia with you around?' she said recklessly. 'I rather doubt it!'

He laughed. 'Flattery, eh?'

'The truth, Seth.' But she could not control a sudden violent shiver, for the cabin was cold and her hair was wet.

He crossed the room, taking an oversized flannelette shirt off a wooden peg. 'This is probably the warmest thing I've got. I'll start the fire while you change.' He took off his boots, then turned his back and began shoving crumpled paper and sticks of kindling into a pot-bellied stove at the other end of the room.

Tascha hung up her jacket and stripped off her nightgown; her whole body was covered with goosebumps. The shirt came almost to her knees, and in width could have encompassed two of her. But it was soft and dry and warm, and its red plaid would hopefully reflect a little colour in her cheeks. Seth was still busy with the fire. She looked around her with interest.

The cabin had plain board walls and a board floor, partially covered by a woven mat. The built-in bunk was perhaps three-quarter size, heaped with Hudson Bay blankets. The table bearing the lamp stood by the window, a shelf above it loaded with books. As a home for two months, the comforts were minimal. But the colours were bright and the crackle of flames cheerful, and, although the rain was drumming on the roof and trickling down the windowpanes, the yellow glow of the oil lamp turned the cabin into a haven from the storm.

The cabin was also very small, thought Tascha; definitely not built for two, one of whom was a large man like Seth. But there was nowhere else in the world she would rather be than with him in this primitive little cabin on the tundra. On her bare feet, she padded across the floor towards the stove, holding out her hands to its first, seeping warmth.

Seth was adjusting the dampers in the metal chimney. He looked down at her and said roughly, 'Your hair's wet—I'll get a brush.'

When he passed it to her, she knelt down by the stove and began running the brush through her hair, holding the long strands to the heat. The firelight through the chinks danced on the blue of her eyes, on the curve of her cheek, on the hair like pale silk. As if he needed violent action, Seth lifted the lid of the stove again, throwing in a couple of logs. The flames leaped upwards. He dropped the lid, then moved away from the stove, saying flatly, 'I'd better get out of here.'

Tascha shook out her hair and slowly got to her feet. Without knowing what she was going to do, she said in a small voice, 'I leave tomorrow, Seth—this is my last night.'

He looked at her sombrely. His back was to the lamp, his face shadowed. 'Yes,' he said.

Her nails dug into her palms. 'Could I stay another week?'

He shook his head. 'It's better that you don't.'

Had he spoken easily, without strain, Tascha might have given up. But the words were forced from him, and she could see the muscles tight along his jaw. 'Because of Belov?' she asked.

'No. That's a side issue, Tascha.'

She felt a thrill of triumph. So the conflict was solely between her and Seth: no outsiders, like Jasmine or Belov. Only the two of them. 'Then why can't I stay?' she asked with assumed calm, for inwardly she felt as if her whole future lay in the balance.

Seth said tightly, 'I own the lodge—I can ask you to leave any time I like.'

'You're not asking Jasmine to leave, and there's surely more provocation there,' she flashed back.

He let his eyes wander over her, from the crown of blonde hair to the slim legs and bare feet. 'I wouldn't use the word provocation, Tascha, if I were you. Not right now.'

The heat that crept up her neck had nothing to do with Tascha's proximity to the stove. She spread her arms so that the shirt stretched out from her body, ludicrously ill-fitting. 'If you find me provocative in this, you must be in love,' she said lightly.

His eyes narrowed; he was patently unamused. 'Don't be ridiculous!'

'So why can't I stay?' she countered. 'You know as well as I do that I earn my keep.'

'That's got nothing to do with it.'

So was Mae right? But Mae was a romantic, and her views on love might be nothing like Seth's. 'When I leave here, will I see you again?'

'As I live in Vancouver and you live in Montreal, I shouldn't think it's likely.'

'You give nothing, do you?' Tascha flared. 'You tell me you want me, and then you stand there like a stick saying we'll never see each other again. Which is the truth, Seth?'

'If you grew up in Pointe Saint-Charles, you must know that life isn't always simple, Tascha. That choices can sometimes be incredibly complicated.'

'One can make one's own complications.' But her temper had died, for the shadow on Seth's face was deep-rooted. 'Seth,' she said quietly, 'do you know what I've wanted all my life and never had? I've wanted to be held, with love. I've wanted to know I matter to someone. That's all. It doesn't seem like much, does it? And yet I've never found it.' She hesitated, then plunged on, for if she was indeed leaving tomorrow she had nothing to lose. 'I—I thought for a while that you might be that someone.'

'Oh, Tascha...' Seth's shoulders were slumped, his voice so low she had to strain to hear it. 'Of all the things you could have asked for, that's the one thing I can't give you. Do you think I haven't realised that there could be something special between us? Of course I have. But I can't act on it, Tascha. I'm afraid to.'

It seemed a supreme irony that the man who had tackled Slim and who had tracked down grizzlies in the wilderness should be afraid of a woman who stood five-foot-six. 'You don't have to be afraid of me, Seth,' she said helplessly.

'I'm afraid of love. I'm afraid of its destructive side, its dark side. Of the power it has to wound and cripple.' He gave a short, humourless laugh. 'What memories I have of its happier side can't counterbalance the rest.'

'Your father and mother,' Tascha said with absolute certainty.

He did not seem surprised that she should know. 'My father loved my mother deeply and unreservedly. But she died, and he never got over it. Love comes at a high price, Tascha. Too high a price. I learned that as a young boy, and it's a lesson I'll never cast off.'

'Have you ever wanted to before?'

'I've never been affected by a woman as I have been by you, no.' He looked up. 'So that's why you should leave, Tascha. Now, before we get any more involved with each other. Because you have your own vulnerabilities, I understand that...and I have no desire to hurt you.'

Knowing she had no choice, she walked towards him, the shirt flapping against her knees. Standing on tiptoes to put her arms around his neck, she kissed his cheek and said quietly, 'Thank you for being honest with me, Seth.'

His eyes roamed her upturned face as if he were trying to memorise every detail of it. Then, making a strangled groan like that of a man driven beyond endurance, he buried his face in the soft clouds of her hair.

Tascha held on to him with all her strength, aching to ease his pain, her own needs lost in his. When he began kissing her, she responded with a generosity that perhaps startled them both; his hands stroked the hair back from her face as his mouth drank deeply of hers. Then, like a man under a spell, he lifted her in his arms and carried her across to the bed.

The blanket was rough against her ankles. As she lay down, he lay beside her, their faces level on the single pillow, so close that his breath stirred her hair. He kissed her again, and in that kiss was all the tenderness that she had craved for years. The rest of the world vanished. Seth was all that mattered, his lips, his hands, his long, lean body.

Through the thick shirt, his hands stroked her breasts, slowly, rhythmically, until she thought she would die with pleasure. He loosened her shirt, pulling it away from her body so that her breasts were exposed to his view. He looked up. Shyness, a touch of fear, and wonderment were all in her face. He kissed her again, then slid his lips to her breast.

The wind keened under the eaves. The rain beat against the roof. But Seth and Tascha were oblivious to the storm outside, for inside the little cabin their own storm was gathering.

Seth had undone the buttons on his own shirt; Tascha rested her cheek against the tangled black hair on his chest and caressed the smoothness of his bare shoulders, touching him in ways she knew she had secretly dreamed of. Her whole body throbbed with desire; her eyes shone with happiness; but most powerful of all was the sense of belonging. She belonged in Seth's arms. She had been fashioned for his lovemaking.

His hand was resting on her breast, his skin rough against hers. 'You're so beautiful,' he murmured. 'I've never seen your body before, yet in a strange way I feel as though I've known it for ever. As though I've been waiting for it for years...'

With a sudden rasp, like a chainsaw running amok, a log scraped down the side of the stove and crashed to the bottom. The snap of sparks overrode even the wind and the rain. Quickly Seth raised himself on one elbow, glancing back over his shoulder at the stove. Tascha waited, a smile on her lips, her cheeks glowing, for she was certain they were going to make love and that she would then belong to Seth in the most real and primitive way there was. She wanted to make love to him. He might be afraid of love, and he had certainly not spoken to her of love, but every touch of his hand, every kiss, seemed suffused with the very emotion he feared.

Seth turned back to her. Her hair was spread on the pillow, her skin as translucent as flower petals and her eyes bluer than the forget-me-nots. He passed a hand across his face. Tascha reached up to touch his wrist. 'What's wrong?' she said softly, for she did not yet understand.

Her fingers were slim, very white against his tanned wrist. With shocking silence, he pulled free. Her hand flopped to the bed. Her eyes widened with dismay. 'Seth?' she faltered.

He sat up, doing up the buttons of his shirt, his hands unsteady. 'I'm going to the lodge,' he muttered. 'We should never have started this, Tascha—it's all wrong.'

Her cry was from the heart. 'It can't be wrong!'

'I can't make love to you, knowing you're leaving tomorrow. I mustn't.' He reached for his boots, shoved his feet into them and began lacing them up.

Tascha sat up, too frightened to realise her shirt was still gaping open. The long curve of Seth's spine and his rumpled hair pierced her to the core, and the words came tumbling out without pride or logic. 'Seth, I want you to make love to me . . . *please*. You can't go! You mustn't leave me alone, not when we were so close, not when I finally knew I belonged—you *can't* take that away from me!'

He tugged his laces tight and stood up, reaching for his jacket. Only when he had it on did he turn around. Tascha's face was panic-stricken, her hands spread in supplication; her body was a pearl-like gleam beneath the heavy shirt. He dragged his eyes away. 'I'll wake you in the morning,' he said hoarsely.

'*Seth!*'

Her voice was ugly with pain; but Seth did not turn around. His boots thudded across the floor. The door squeaked open on its hinges, then swung shut behind him. she heard the rattle of the latch, then nothing but the wind, the rain, and the mutter of the fire.

She pulled the shirt about her body, her face pinched. He had gone. He had left her alone. But, cruellest of all, he had given her that sense of belonging she had always longed for, and then had ripped it from her. Had she remained ignorant, she might never have missed it ... but in showing her all that she had lacked, he had sown the seeds of a most bitter deprivation.

She fell back on the bed, buried her face in the pillow, and wept.

CHAPTER EIGHT

THE window at the foot of the bunk in Seth's cabin faced east, so Tascha woke to a bright flood of sunshine on her face. Even before she opened her eyes, she knew where she was. In Seth's bed. In Seth's cabin. On the morning when she had to leave him.

As she burrowed into the pillow, it seemed to her that she caught the elusive scent of his body, and she knew as certainly as she had ever known anything that she wanted him here with her in the bed. Perhaps because she had so often felt like an outsider at school and university, not part of the group, she had also wondered about her own sexuality, wondering if there, too, she would always be the outsider, the odd one out. Certainly, she had never felt impelled into anyone's bed. Not until she had met Seth.

She hugged the pillow to her, knowing she would be losing something precious and irreplaceable if she left here today and never saw Seth again. She could hide, she thought wildly. When it was time for the bus to depart for the airstrip, she would hide in the rafters of the woodshed, among the old sleeping-bags and air mattresses and rubber tyres that were bundled away up there. She would not climb meekly on to the bus and allow herself to be driven away from a place that freed her spirit and from a man to whom in some strange way she belonged...

But here pragmatism asserted itself. She had to help Mae with breakfast and then she would have to pack, and she would not put it past Seth to keep a close eye on her. Besides, the door of the woodshed was in full view of the lodge.

Suddenly unable to bear being in Seth's bed any longer, she threw back the blankets and sat up. The quiet struck her. No howling wind, no drumming rain. Only the silent stream of sunshine over the bed.

She scrambled to the floor, made the bed, put on her sneakers and jacket and left the cabin without a backward look. She ran to her tent as fast as she could, Seth's shirt bunched around her knees, and fortunately met no one. Her carry-all contained one pair of jeans that were only slightly damp, and from a mixture of motives she left on the big plaid shirt. Then she left her tent and headed for the lodge.

The sik-siks were out in full force. Droplets of rain that were caught in the lichens and grasses sparkled in the sun like a shower of carelessly flung jewels; each rose-pink flower of the willow-herb carried a jewel in its centre. The mountains were stark against the sky. The air smelled clean and crisp, newly washed.

Tascha took a deep breath of that air, her blue eyes fierce with resolve. She couldn't leave today...she wouldn't! She would have to play her last card and tell Seth about her suspicions that Belov might be her father and Marya her mother. In her bag, she had copies of the two letters. She would show him those letters and beg him not to send her away.

She should have done it sooner. But she had shrunk from exposing her hopes, her nakedness of spirit, to another person. Easier by far, she thought wryly, to expose her body than her soul.

With renewed purpose, Tascha hurried to the lodge. But although the clock said twenty to seven she was there before Mae, the first time that had happened since she had arrived. Luckily, she knew the routine. She turned on the oven, hearing the pop of the gas as it ignited, and began taking out the ingredients for bran muffins.

At seven o'clock when the first batch of muffins was in the oven, Mae still had not arrived. Tascha was worried by now, for Mae took her duties at the lodge very seriously and was punctual to a degree. She set the timer for the muffins and left the kitchen, jogging across the grass to Mae's little cabin, which was at the opposite end of the complex of buildings from Seth's. She tapped on the door. 'Mae? Are you there?'

From inside, a voice wavered, 'Is that you, dear?'

Tascha opened the door. Mae was still in bed, the green twill curtains drawn against the morning light. Her cheeks were flushed and her grey curls in disarray. Alarmed, Tascha said, 'Are you ill?'

Mae let her head fall back on the pillow. 'That's right, dear. Will you tell Seth?'

'Of course I will—and I'll bring you over some breakfast.'

'Just a glass of juice. Nothing to eat.'

'Seth will make a fire for you, too. Do you think it's the 'flu, Mae?'

'Didn't feel myself yesterday, I have to admit...can you manage dinner on your own, dear?'

'But, Mae, I'm leaving today!'

Mae's voice was perceptibly firmer. 'You won't be able to leave. There's no one else to cook dinner. Seth has to drive the bus for the new guests, and Martin can't cook an egg.'

Unconsciously, Tascha was wringing her hands. 'Martin could drive the bus and Seth cook dinner.'

Mae shook her head. 'Seth always takes the old guests out and brings the new ones in. They expect it.'

Although hope was burgeoning in Tascha's breast, she said, 'Seth doesn't want me to stay, Mae.'

'He'll have to lump it,' Mae announced. 'I can't help being sick and the guests have to eat. So that's that.'

That indeed was that. Tascha said at random, 'One of the reasons he doesn't want me to stay is because I'm looking for Andrei Belov.'

Mae frowned. 'Is that why you want to stay?'

'Partly.' With deep relief, Tascha finally spoke the truth. 'Mae, there's a chance Belov could be my father— I have to find him!'

'Never heard he had any family,' Mae remarked, then looked nonplussed. 'Now look what you made me say!' she complained fractiously. 'Seth'll half kill me.'

If Mae hadn't been ill, Tascha might have laughed. 'I won't tell him, I promise.'

'Is that man Belov the only reason you want to stay?'

Again, Tascha opted for the truth. 'No. There's Seth, as well. Because I think you were right about him being afraid.'

Had the curtains not been drawn so tightly, Tascha might have seen a gleam of satisfaction in Mae's eyes. But all Mae said was, 'You'd better get busy with the breakfast, dear, or you'll be late.' Then she pulled the covers up to her chin and turned her face to the wall.

Tascha crept out of the cabin, closed the door as quietly as she could, then raced across the grass to the lodge, feeling as though she was floating, she was so happy. She could stay at the lodge...she did not have to leave! She burst in the back door. The timer she had set was ringing madly and the kitchen reeked of burned muffins. Seth was standing by the stove, holding the pan.

Tascha came to an abrupt halt, although she could not quite wipe the idiotic grin from her face. 'You might as well feed those to the ravens,' she said.

Seth scowled at her. 'Where the hell is everyone? I come over here and the kitchen's full of smoke and that stupid bell's sounding the last trump.'

She turned off the timer. But because she knew she was staying and because her whole body still felt light with happiness, Tascha smiled at him without the slightest touch of repentance. 'So fire me,' she said impudently.

He took a step closer, still clutching the muffin pan. 'Why are you looking so damned pleased with yourself?' he demanded.

'Mae's sick. I don't mean I'm happy that she's sick, but it means I'll have to stay. To cook dinner.' And again a smile split her face.

'Mae's never sick!'

'Well, she's sick today. I told her you'd go over and light a fire to warm up the cabin. You can take her some orange juice at the same time.'

'You're great at giving orders.' Seth banged the tin of muffins on the counter. 'We'll have a cold supper tonight—so you won't have to stay.'

Tascha said airily, 'And will you bake three pies for dessert and make the bread for tomorrow's lunch? Or will Martin?'

'You're enjoying this, aren't you?' Seth said furiously.

Tascha raised her chin. 'Yes. Because I'd just about reached the point where I was going to hide in the attic of the woodshed so I wouldn't have to leave.'

Seth's expression was as nonplussed as Mae's when she had made the slip about Belov. 'I give you full marks for determination,' he said finally.

She widened her eyes innocently. 'But not for my muffins.'

He did not laugh. 'You've really got me, haven't you, Tascha?' he grated. 'You've won. You can stay. I hope you're happy.'

'*You* don't look very happy. Come on, Seth, crack a smile.'

Nothing even approaching a smile crossed Seth's face. 'You might have won the battle, but you haven't won the war,' he said astringently. 'Because nothing has changed, Tascha—there'll be no more episodes like last night.'

Her happiness was dimmed like sun behind a cloud. 'As I have to produce breakfast for fifteen people in less than an hour, I hardly think this is the time for a discussion about last night.'

'I didn't say we were going to discuss it—I said it wouldn't happen again.'

'Oh, go away, Seth!' Tascha cried in exasperation. 'I've got work to do.'

He threw a nasty smile over his shoulder as he went to the refrigerator for the orange juice. 'You certainly have—you might be sorry that you stayed. Before I come back with the new group of guests, all the beds have to be changed, the linen and towels washed, and the cabins dusted and swept. Besides baking bread for tomorrow's lunch and three pies.' He raised the glass of juice to her in ironic salute and left via the back door.

None of Tascha's vocabulary seemed adequate for her present emotional state. She fired the muffins out onto the grass for the ravens and got to work.

Tascha's tent had never looked as good as it did at nine-thirty that night. In the midst of all the chores that Seth had outlined, she had found time to hang out her sleeping-bag and her clothes to dry, a rather miraculous feat of memory, she thought now, as she climbed into the bag. She had also found time to say goodbye to the departing guests and to be introduced to the new arrivals, whose cabins were all ready and waiting for them. Dinner had been half an hour late, but she had made three chocolate cream pies, and the ham and scallops had disappeared rapidly enough that she had been re-assured about her culinary abilities.

Lying on her back in the sleeping-bag, Tascha crossed her hands behind her head, trying to ease the ache between her shoulders. Dinner had brought a major surprise. She had caught glimpses of Jasmine that morning, enough to see that the girl looked chastened and was avoiding Seth as diligently as she had earlier pursued him; but Jasmine and Clyde, who were staying for another week, had both gone along for the drive to the airstrip. Clyde had spotted two gyrfalcons and a marsh hawk on the return trip, so he was happy. Jasmine had added nothing to this conversation. But, as Tascha was flying around the kitchen trying to get everything served at once, Jasmine had approached the hatch and said diffidently, 'Where's Mae?'

'She's sick,' Tascha replied, lifting the lid of the scallops and poking the potatoes to see if they were done.

'Oh. I could help if you like.'

Tascha almost dropped the lid of the saucepan, glad that her back was to Jasmine so the girl could not see her expression of stunned surprise. She flung a smile over her shoulder and said heartily, 'Sure! I'd appreciate some help.'

Jasmine was quick-witted and seemed to regard the array of saucepans and dishes as a challenge. Side by side, she and Tascha strained vegetables, carved the ham and arranged it on a platter, then put out the plates, the spinach salad, the water and milk jugs and the relish.

Tascha, whose face was scarlet from the heat of the stove, said sincerely, 'Thanks, Jasmine.'

Jasmine gave her a sideways smile and slipped out of the kitchen. Although she did not offer to help clean up afterwards, Tascha did not mind, for the few minutes of camaraderie in the kitchen had been an immense step forward.

Now she tried to keep her eyes open to think about
Seth and plan a strategy as far as Belov was concerned;
but they insisted on closing and by ten o'clock she was
sound asleep.

Although Mae was still feeling peaky, as she put it, on
Monday, Tascha found the day almost like a holiday
after the mad rush of Sunday. The new guests appeared
to have settled in, and Jasmine helped put out the lunch
ingredients as well as serve up the dinner. Clyde was so
openly amazed by the transformation in his daughter
that Tascha found herself avoiding him, not wanting to
disturb the delicate balance between herself and Jasmine
by discussing Jasmine's behaviour with Clyde. She would
not have avoided Seth had he shown any preference for
her company; but Seth was doing a very thorough job
of ignoring her presence.

On Tuesday, Mae appeared in the kitchen in time to
help with lunch preparations, and pronounced herself
recuperated sufficiently to get dinner with Tascha. Tascha
insisted on cleaning up the breakfast dishes, however,
not wanting Mae to tire herself. When she had finished,
she walked back to her tent. There were only patches of
blue sky today, peeking through dark-edged clouds, and
rain-squalls had clustered on the horizon. But rain, she
now knew, meant rainbows.

She had been in her tent perhaps ten minutes when
the first drops struck the roof. Her bed was now placed
in the exact centre of the tent; she sat on it cross-legged,
smug in the knowledge that she would stay dry. The
squall lasted only a few minutes. When it was over,
Tascha put on boots and went outside.

A rainbow hung in a glistening arc over the lodge.
Tascha followed its graceful curve to its ending in a pond
out on the barrens. But if she were to walk towards that
pond the rainbow would retreat, always out of reach,

nebulous, unable to be grasped. Like Seth, her mind whispered, as her gaze came back towards the lodge.

As if she had conjured him up, she saw him standing just outside his cabin door, looking skyward. With a pang of her heart, she knew she wanted to run down the slope towards him and clasp him in her arms to feel his reality, so different from the shimmering illusion of the rainbow. Then the truth struck her, vibrant as the prismatic colours in the sky. I'm in love with him, she thought dazedly. I love Seth. He's the real reason I didn't want to leave the lodge—I couldn't bear the thought of never seeing him again.

She felt an instant of perfect peace, for in recognising that she loved Seth she had discovered both her ability to love and the joy that love brings; and that peace was bound up in the beauty of the rainbow against the cloudy sky. But then the tableau changed. Seth moved, starting up the slope towards her. He saw her, checked, then picked up his stride.

Panic usurped peace. Mae's illness had brought her another week, Tascha thought, but that was all. Two days of that week had already passed, and in those two days she and Seth had scarcely spoken to one another. She had to do something. But what?

Seth was already angling away from her tent and heading for the bus, where, she saw in a quick glance over her shoulder, the guests were gathering for the daily hike. He would be gone all day. She would be busy in the kitchen when he came back, and then he could easily spend the evening in the observation lounge with the guests. 'Seth!' she cried, and impulsively gestured to him with one hand.

He did not bother to hide the reluctance with which he slowed his steps. She ran across the grass towards him, stopped two feet away from him, and saw that his face was closed against her, like a door shut tight. She bit her lip, for the peace and joy she had felt were powerless against his implacable features. 'What is it?' he said with impersonal brevity.

'I—I need to talk to you,' she stammered.

He eyed her distraught face. 'Don't tell me *you're* getting the 'flu now.'

Her chin snapped up. 'What do you mean?'

'I mean Mae's little illness was very conveniently timed.'

'Are you insinuating she faked it?' Tascha said incredulously.

'She could have, yes...or the two of you could have concocted it between you.'

'We did *not*!' Tascha flared. 'What a horrible mind you have, Seth Curtis.'

'I distrust coincidence, that's all. Did you want something, Tascha?'

Not sure whether she loved him or hated him, Tascha repeated, 'I need to talk to you.'

'I'm already behind schedule,' he said shortly. 'I didn't want to leave while it was raining.'

'This evening then.'

He gave her a long, considering look during which she wondered what she would do if he refused. 'Nine o'clock,' he said. 'I'll meet you by the gate.'

She watched him walk towards the guests and could picture the affable smile on his lips. Hypocrite, she seethed. Hateful man! How dared he accuse her of collaborating with Mae! Although, she thought with reluctant justice, he could be correct in his assessment of Mae's convenient illness. Mae was a romantic. Mae might very well want to throw Tascha and Seth together and, if an attack of the 'flu would accomplish that, then Mae would get the 'flu. The flush on her cheeks could well have been rouge, and the green curtains had been closely enough drawn to discourage scrutiny. Certainly

Mae had recovered quite rapidly once the bus had departed for the airstrip...

Ten minutes later, when the guests had left, Tascha went for a walk by herself. She already knew what she was going to say to Seth that evening, so her mind was free to wander over all the contradictions in his nature and, more earthily, over her very clear memories of their lovemaking. A gyrfalcon flew overhead and her boot was within two feet of a rare species of gentian, and she saw neither one.

Dinner was considerably easier to prepare with Mae's sturdy presence beside her. Mae made no references to her illness and Tascha certainly lacked the courage to enquire as to its origin. If Mae, who knew Seth well, had thought it worth while to deceive him, then it was up to her, Tascha, to take advantage of that deception.

Nine o'clock found Tascha wandering towards the gate, wearing a becoming pink shirt and quite a lot of perfume. The gate was in full view of the observation lounge; it would be impossible for her and Seth to indulge in either a blazing row or a passionate embrace. She was sure he knew that. She thrust her hands in the pockets of her jeans and stared moodily at the mountains, resenting their magisterial calm.

At four minutes past nine, Seth sauntered down to the gate. He was wearing a khaki shirt, a down waistcoat and jeans. He said, 'We just sighted a herd of nine or ten caribou in the direction of Manning Peak. They must be gathering for the fall migration.'

His casual remark touched on the passage of time and the coming of winter. Leaning on the gatepost, Tascha said quickly, before she could lose her courage, 'Seth, you said the other night that my search for Belov was only a side issue. That may be true. But I'd still like to tell you why it's important that I speak to him.'

Seth looked momentarily disconcerted; perhaps, she thought with a touch of sly humour, he had been expecting her to proposition him. But at least he did not attempt to deny Belov's existence. 'Why don't you?' he said agreeably.

She searched his face for any sign of sarcasm, found none, and said, 'There's a chance—an outside chance— that he might be my father.'

She had Seth's full attention; he looked stunned rather than disconcerted. 'That's impossible,' he said flatly. 'I'd have known about it.'

Her smile was ironic. 'It was a long time ago, Seth— over twenty years.'

'My father would have told me.'

'Not necessarily. I had, after all, supposedly died.'

'It sounds to me as though you've been reading too many books about Anastasia,' he said nastily. 'Andrei Belov, in his own way, is a very famous man.'

'Don't, Seth, please,' Tascha said, and put her hand on his arm, touching him for the first time since they had been together in the cabin. The dark hair under her fingertips was unexpectedly smooth; his skin was warm. She fought down a wave of such fierce desire that she was left inwardly trembling, and said in a low voice, desperate with sincerity, 'I'm not interested in his fame. Nor in his money. I only want to know, Seth. I *have* to know.'

Seth said in a non-committal voice, 'You told me your mother died recently.'

'She might not have been my mother.' Tascha grasped the gatepost with both hands, her nails digging into the wood; her blue eyes were fixed on the mountains. 'It's a terrible thing to say, but I almost wish she weren't. She never loved me, Seth—never! There were lots of times I think she hated me, and it was never anything I said or did. It was just—me. She'd look at me as though she saw someone else standing there, and her eyes would be like flint, cold and sharp, filled with hate and bitterness... and because she never loved me, I could never love her. All my life I've felt guilty because I couldn't love the woman I thought was my mother. So, when I found the letters after she died, I got on a plane and came out here without even thinking. I had to come.' Abruptly, she ran out of words.

'Letters?' Seth repeated sharply.

'After Olga died, I had to go through her personal belongings.' She gave a reminiscent shiver, for such had been Olga's personality that the whole time Tascha had been sorting and boxing the meagre effects she had felt Olga watching her, inimical, resentful of such a disturbance of her privacy. 'There were two letters at the back of one of her drawers, both postmarked Whitehorse, both dated twenty years ago. The only signature on the letters was Belov. But he talked of a child and of a woman called Marya... maybe Marya was my mother, Seth.'

Seth put a hand on the tense line of Tascha's shoulder. 'I can see why you would want her to be... Have you got the letters with you, Tascha?'

She blinked rapidly, because his gesture of understanding had brought tears to her eyes. 'I only brought copies of them—I was afraid I might lose them.'

'Will you show them to me?'

She nodded imperceptibly, shoved her hands in her pockets and led the way towards her tent. The letters were carefully stored in a zippered pocket in her carryall. She took them out, went outside to where Seth was waiting, and passed them to him.

He read each of them twice, frowning slightly, taking his time, until she thought she would scream with suspense. Then he looked over at her and his eyes were full of compassion. 'They're very persuasive,' he said. 'And I'd probably have done the same thing as you—jumped on a plane and come out here as quickly as I could. But there's something I haven't told you, Tascha. You see, I once asked Andrei if he had any family...it wasn't that long ago. Maybe two years. He smiled at me—he has grey eyes that seem to have seen everything under the sun—and said, "No, I have no family."' Slowly Seth folded the letters. 'He had no reason to lie to me, Tascha. We've been friends for years.'

An ice-cold hand seemed to be squeezing her heart. 'Perhaps he's forgotten me,' she whispered. 'It's a long time ago.'

'I don't think Andrei has ever forgotten anything he's seen or done—that's one of his gifts as a writer.'

'But the letters!' Tascha cried helplessly.

With crisp logic, Seth said, 'If the letters are true, Olga lied to Belov about his child's death and to you about your parentage. That's wicked, any way you look at it. Perhaps she wrote the letters herself twenty years ago. Perhaps they referred to other Russian immigrants, nothing to do with you. Perhaps there were two children, the one who died—and you.'

Battered by his words, Tascha lowered her head, no longer able to think coherently, only able to feel. The world seemed to have shifted under her feet, leaving her floating, weightless, tied to no one, belonging nowhere.

Seth said urgently, 'Don't look like that, Tascha. You don't need Belov or Marya or Olga. You're a woman of courage and passion and independence, you're beautiful, you're intelligent...you'll make your own niche in the world and perhaps because of your upbringing you'll never accept things at face-value. At twenty-two, you've learned things some people never learn.'

'But I'll never know who I am!' she cried.

'You're yourself,' he said fiercely.

'Oh, sure...but I don't matter to anyone.'

'You matter enough to me to get past all the barriers I've ever built up. You keep me awake at night because I want to make love to you. You haunt my dreams when I sleep.'

She swayed towards him. 'Seth...'

His kiss was a single passionate outburst. Then he thrust her away, his eyes burning in their sockets. 'I can't be near you without wanting you,' he said bitterly.

And because he was looking at her as if he hated her, just as Olga had, Tascha backed away, clutching the letters like a talisman, the knowledge of her love for him a leaden weight in her breast. She said incoherently, 'I've taken up enough of your time. Thank you for listening. Goodnight, Seth.' And she scurried into her tent with more haste than dignity. He did not come after her. She heard his footsteps retreat in the direction of the lodge, then the silence of the tundra resumed itself, undisturbed.

CHAPTER NINE

TASCHA slept poorly, the metal cot creaking each time she turned over, the tent flapping in the breeze like luffing sails. She got up at six, feeling tired and out of sorts, hoping that the view from the tent would restore her equanimity. But the sweep of tundra and the distant majesty of the mountains made her feel small and insignificant, rather than serene, and she had forgotten to put water outside the night before to wash her face and clean her teeth. She retreated into her tent, got dressed, and set off in the direction of the lodge.

Early as she was, someone was up before her: Seth. He was loading something in the back of the jeep, which was parked by the woodshed. Tascha fell back a little, not ready to talk to anyone yet, least of all Seth. He lifted a small haversack into the jeep, then headed diagonally away from the jeep, back towards his cabin.

Tascha stood very still, concealed from him by a sprawling sik-sik burrow and a clump of willow shrubs. He passed close enough that she could see the frown of concentration on his face and the inwardly turned eyes. He did not see her.

She waited until he was out of sight. Then, without stopping to analyse her motives, she ran towards the jeep. The hatch had been left open. A heavily loaded backpack and a smaller haversack were lying against the spare tyre and a crumpled piece of canvas tarpaulin. Her fingers nimble with haste, she unbuckled the backpack. It was full of food supplies.

Quickly, she slid the worn leather strap back through the buckle, every nerve straining for the sound of Seth's return. She backed away from the jeep with attempted casualness, then ran for the kitchen door.

She had the kitchen to herself. She stood by the window, looking out, and the thoughts clicked through her brain like the program on a computer screen. Seth's backpack, which was full of food, was in the jeep. He had loaded the jeep at a time when he would expect to be undetected. If he delegated Martin to take the guests for their daily hike, then the inevitable conclusion was that he was heading out to see Belov.

Without her.

We'll see about that! thought Tascha, feeling the stirrings of rage; and she was still standing by the window when Mae pushed open the kitchen door. 'Morning, dear,' said Mae.

Tascha turned to face her, her blue eyes burning with purpose. 'Mae, I might have to leave in a hurry this morning—will you cover for me?'

Mae blinked. 'Now, where would you be going?'

'I'd rather you didn't ask. I don't want to tell you the truth, and I don't want to lie, either.'

'So it's to do with Seth,' said Mae. 'Sure, I'll cover for you, dear.'

Impulsively, Tascha gave Mae a hug. 'You're a sweetheart—thanks!' she said, then set to work with a will.

Seth ate breakfast with the guests before announcing, not at all to Tascha's surprise, that Martin would be taking them out for the day. Tascha winked at Mae and slipped out of the back door. The hatch was closed on the jeep. She opened it with exquisite care, climbed in the back, and latched it shut. The tarpaulin was fortunately quite large and, also fortunately, was positioned behind the driver's seat. She spread it out a little more, then crawled underneath.

The canvas smelled musty, the light seeping through it in a dull orange glow. The floor of the jeep was made of ridged metal, and was both cold and hard. Tascha curled up and hoped sincerely that Seth would not be long.

She had scarcely arranged her knees against the hub cap, and rested her cheek on her hand, when the jeep door opened, the sound muffled by the heavy folds of the tarpaulin. The springs settled a little as someone, presumably Seth, climbed in. The door slammed shut. The engine was started and the jeep began bumping across the ground.

Tascha clutched the tarp around her, wishing she had brought a blanket to lie on to lessen the direct relationship between the bumps in the road and her anatomy. She braced herself as the jeep reached the edge of the driveway; then the vehicle teetered again as Seth hit one of the deep ruts caused by the last rainstorm. He, of course, was cushioned by the seat. No reason why he should avoid the ruts. She gritted her teeth and wondered what she would do if by any chance Seth was not going to visit Belov. Throw a tantrum?

The next half-hour was not a time Tascha ever chose to remember. She had read of men who went over Niagara Falls in barrels and had always thought they must be crazy; she now knew they were. But eventually, when she had almost reached the point of flinging off the tarpaulin to sit in the passenger seat regardless of the consequences, she felt the jeep turn sharply to the left and skid down a steep incline. Pebbles rolled under the tyres, rather than gravel or mud. The riverbed, she thought with a quiver of excitement. They had arrived at the creek which marked the end of the road.

The jeep braked to a halt. The engine was turned off. The driver's door opened, then banged shut, and Tascha heard the crunch of footsteps coming round the jeep to the hatch door. She tensed every muscle and closed her eyes. Just like an ostrich, she thought foolishly, and heard the hatch squeal open, the backpack slide across the floor, and a grunt of exertion as Seth heaved the pack on to his back. The hatch closed. Stones rattled underfoot in a decrescendo. Then silence.

A fold of canvas had wedged itself against her face in the descent to the creek, almost suffocating her. Very carefully, Tascha raised one hand and pushed it away. Nothing happened. No one yelled at her. No one pulled the tarpaulin away and demanded to know what she was doing. Emboldened, she pushed her head free of the canvas altogether, and peered around her, her neck muscles protesting violently. Both seats were empty. The silence continued unbroken. Very slowly, she raised her head to the level of the windows, just in time to see Seth—black head over a loaded backpack—disappear into a gully. He had already travelled an astonishing distance away from the jeep.

Cursing herself for being overcautious, Tascha struggled free of the tarpaulin, flipped the latch on the hatch door and jumped to the ground. Between her and the ridge of hills that they had climbed to find the Arctic poppies, was another, lower line of hills covered with shrubs and lichen; the creek babbled in the distance. She began walking swiftly in the direction Seth had taken.

She was in a narrow valley, its floor a tumble of rounded boulders that reflected the early morning warmth of the sun. Tascha took off her jacket, knotting it around her waist, and glanced up at the cloudless sky. An eagle was circling high overhead. She took it as a good omen and pressed on, knowing she could not afford to lose Seth, a little frightened by the prospect that she might. There was no road to keep to here, as there had been when she had followed Eddie; not even a trail.

She reached the gully and saw Seth straight ahead of her, a small figure threading its way through the waist-high willows that had sprouted among the rocks. She tried to walk faster.

She was soon breathing hard. Her outermost sweater joined her jacket around her waist, leaving her in a short-sleeved T-shirt. Her sneakers were not the best of footwear for climbing over rocks at high speed; she vowed if she ever returned to the north she would buy the most expensive hiking boots available, and pushed on.

Seth passed behind a low green hillock. Tascha tried to increase her speed again, careless of the noise she made. The willow branches whipped against her legs and scratched her arms; a mosquito whined in her ear, and on the hillside a flock of birds twittered and chirped. She came to the hillock and rounded it. The ground dropped as the valley widened into a rock-strewn plain, as if long ago a glacier had crept that far and then retreated.

The plain was empty. She could not see Seth.

Tascha felt a surge of pure terror, for it seemed to her overwrought imagination that he had vanished as the rainbow vanishes when you approach it too closely. Then she quelled her fear, noticing that the rocky plain sloped downwards at its far perimeter. Seth had walked down that slope, she told herself firmly. He had not disappeared into thin air.

But as she crossed the plain her eyes darted from side to side in case he had turned to either the right or the left to climb up one of the gullies carved by long-ago streams between the low hills. She saw no sign of him and pressed on, tamping down the panic that persisted in nibbling away at her confidence. The land was so vast, so uncaring, and a human being in contrast such a puny thing. She could disappear here and never be heard of again, she thought uneasily, for it would take an army of searchers to trace every crevasse and beat every hillside.

When the plain sloped downwards, the valley took another twist; from the air, Tascha decided, the valley must curve in S-bends like a mighty grey river. But the bend revealed green, not grey, the green of grass, as if the glacier had ground rocks to earth and the earth had borne seed like a miniature Garden of Eden. Tascha found herself smiling, for the green hollow was beautiful; and there was a single row of fresh tracks leading across the grass.

She began following the tracks, relishing the grass's softness, breathing in the elusive scent from its bruised blades. Because her footsteps were almost soundless, the sudden splash of water came clearly to her ears. She slowed, puzzled, for the sound was nothing like the steady rush of a creek. It was as if someone—or something—was swimming.

Grizzlies like to swim, she thought, with a vague recollection of a photograph of a grizzly up to its haunches in a river in one of the books in the lounge. Sweat sprang out on her palms. She crept towards the screen of willows that lay between her and the mysterious splashing. Crouched low, she peered through the shiny oval leaves.

A small lake lay in front of her, edged with pale sand and tall, curving rushes whose reflection shimmered in the sun. The swimmer was Seth, his black hair clinging sleekly to his scalp, his strong arms flashing as he cleaved the crystal-clear water. She sank back on her heels, forgetting all her fears, absorbed in the simple pleasure of watching the man she loved.

He was enjoying himself, she could tell. Had she not been hiding from him, she would have liked to join him. He swam for perhaps another two or three minutes. Then

he reared up from the lake and walked straight towards
her, water flying in all directions. He was stark naked.

With a gasp of dismay, she tried to back out of the
bushes, tripped on a root and landed heavily on her
behind. Like an animal that freezes at the scent of
danger, Seth stopped dead. 'Who's there?' he called.

A flush of humiliation scorched Tascha's cheeks, for
she had been caught like a peeping Tom. Now that it
was too late, she saw the haversack and the pile of clothes
on the beach; she could have guessed he would not bother
with swimming trunks. Slowly, she stood up.

'Who is it?' Seth repeated sharply, and she only then
realised that he could not see her through the thick green
willows; that he, like herself, might be afraid of grizzlies. She pushed her way through the shrubbery,
branches snapping as she went, and stumbled on to the
beach. He was about four feet away from her. Knowing
her cheeks must be scarlet, she kept her eyes trained on
his face, and could not think of a thing to say.

For perhaps five seconds Seth stared back. Then,
without hurry, he bent, took his jeans from the pile of
clothing, and pulled them up his hips. The sound of the
zipper was excruciatingly loud, for the rippled lake was
subsiding to smoothness and there was not a breath of
wind. He said without inflection, 'Where the hell did
you come from?'

'I was hidden in the back of the jeep.'

'Following me.'

It was a statement, not a question. 'Yes.'

'Figuring I'd lead you to Belov.' There was an edge
of menace under the quietly spoken words.

Her throat had gone dry, so she merely nodded. He
said, 'You're never content to let events unfold, are you,
Tascha? You've always got to be hurrying them along.'

Her nostrils flared. She was suddenly furious, a fury
fed by the memory of his lean, tanned body silhouetted

against the lake. She said tightly, 'Deny that you're going to see Belov.'

'That's exactly where I'm going. Or was, until you appeared.'

'No, Seth. You're going to see him and you'll take me with you,' she replied, keeping her voice flat with an immense effort.

'I won't do that, Tascha. Not——'

Her control snapped. 'You will *not* keep me from my father!' she exploded. 'You will *not*!'

He closed the distance between them and seized her by the shoulders. 'I have to——'

'I've come thousands of miles to find him,' she raged. 'I'm not getting this close without seeing him, Seth Curtis, do you hear me? I won't allow you to keep me away from him—you have no right to do that! Maybe he's not my father...maybe he's just a creation of my fantasies. But I have to find out. I *will* find out!' And she stamped her foot in fury on the yielding sand.

Seth shook her, looking every bit as angry as she. 'Will you kindly listen to me?' he shouted.

'I'm tired of listening to you!' she yelled back. 'You've been obstructing me since the first time I met you. Lying to me. Trying to keep me from the man who might be my father—acting like God. Don't you see what it means to me, Seth? Don't you understand at all?' In sudden, bitter anguish, she closed her eyes against the dazzling brilliance of the sun. Her anger collapsed. Her body went boneless in his grasp, limp as a rag doll. As she dropped her head to her chest, the sun caught in the strands of her hair, gleaming like gold.

Wordlessly, Seth drew her towards him, putting his arms around her and holding her to his bare, wet chest. 'Tascha, I understand,' he said gently. 'I've understood ever since you showed me the letters and told me about Olga.'

Her voice muffled against his skin, she cried, 'Then why won't you take me to him?'

'Perhaps I should have told you last night what I planned to do today. But it seemed cruel to raise your hopes...to keep you in suspense all day.' With one hand he was rhythmically stroking her drooping shoulders. 'You're trembling,' he said helplessly. 'I'm sorry, Tascha, I didn't mean to hurt you again. I was trying to shield you from hurt.'

Nothing he was saying made sense to her; only the slow movements of his hand seemed real. She looked up, her eyes glazed with unshed tears. 'I don't know what you're talking about, Seth.'

'Andrei Belov isn't a young man,' Seth said, choosing his words with care. 'From the little my father told me, I gather he had a hard life in Russia before he escaped—he spent years in exile, and some months in a labour camp. He drives himself unmercifully when he's writing; and my father's death hit him hard. I didn't feel I could take you to see him without preparing him first, Tascha. Let's say you are his daughter...the shock would be immense. So today I was going to broach the subject to him, describe you and tell him about the two letters. Then, assuming he agreed to see you, he'd at least be prepared.'

What Seth was saying did make sense to her now. Tascha scrubbed the tears from her eyes and faltered, 'I—I'm sorry I yelled at you.'

He smiled. 'I yelled, too. With less reason.' He reached up and smoothed her hair. 'What you've got to understand is that Andrei lives like a hermit. He's the most self-sufficient man I know. He doesn't dislike people—in fact, among a few trusted friends he can be highly gregarious—but most of the time he can do without them. And he loathes publicity. So I honestly believe it would be better if today I paved the way for you.'

'Perhaps he won't want to see me.'

'I'll do the very best for you that I can, Tascha.'

Intuitively she believed him, for Seth, once having given his word, would not go back on it. She rested her palms lightly on his chest, her blue eyes without artifice, and said, 'I'm truly sorry for losing my temper.'

He smiled back, his face unguarded. 'You're forgiven.'

She glanced down and saw her hands resting on his chest, entangled in the dark hair, and felt against her palm the heavy stroke of his heartbeat. She snatched her hands away as if they were burning and retreated a step. 'I'd better go back to the jeep,' she muttered, unable to meet his eyes.

But Seth took her hands in his and brought them back to lie against his chest. He was no longer smiling. 'Don't go. Not yet.'

She was agonisingly aware of his closeness and, at some deep level, frightened of giving in to that closeness. She said, with a valiant attempt at matter-of-factness, 'Shouldn't I wait for you in the jeep rather than here?'

He ignored her question. Her hands were now captured in only one of his; with the other he was smoothing her hair again, as if its fairness fascinated him. When he spoke, his voice was low and reflective. 'I've been coming here since I was a kid,' he said. 'I suppose I was about eight or nine when I first saw this lake, and I thought it was the most beautiful place in the world. A miniature paradise. An oasis in the northern desert. As I got older, I used to fantasise that someday I would meet the perfect woman here.' His eyes warmed with self-deprecatory laughter towards that younger Seth. 'She was always unimaginably beautiful, a combination of Ingrid Bergman and Ann-Margret. But I can't recall that she had much personality.' He tweaked Tascha's hair. 'So here I am today with you—the only woman who's ever been here with me. You're foolhardy and impetuous and opinionated, and you tell me off when I need it . . . not quite the ethereal creature I had in mind.'

'Reality versus fantasy,' Tascha murmured, fluttering her lashes at him.

'I must admit you're a lot more interesting. Worship and adulation can only go so far—which is not to say I don't find you distractingly beautiful, Tascha.'

She was sure he had meant to speak lightly; but in spite of himself his voice had roughened and the hand clasping hers had tightened around her fingers. Trying to keep her gaze anywhere but on the expanse of bare flesh right in front of her nose, she said, 'I have a hard time picturing Ingrid Bergman at the Scagway Tavern.'

Again, she might as well have spoken to the four winds. 'Kiss me, Tascha,' Seth said and lowered his head. She closed her eyes and complied.

It was a kiss that seemed to last a very long time, at the end of which she was locked in his arms, his hands kneading her spine under her shirt, hers caressing the nape of his neck and the dark, springy hair. He released her mouth to rain kisses on her closed lids and the silken slide of her cheek, then tugged at the ribbon that was holding her hair in a ponytail. The ribbon fell to the sand and her hair floated loosely about her face and shoulders. He ran his hands through it so it cascaded over his wrists, then tugged her forwards to kiss him again. Against her mouth he murmured, 'I want to make love to you.'

She wanted the same, but might not have found the courage to say so. 'I'm real—not fantasy,' she warned him gravely.

'It is *you*, Tascha, whom I want. The real woman,' he said, and the words were like a vow.

It seemed absolutely right to her that they make love outdoors on the grassy shore of a lake as clear as glass; but she had no idea how to begin. She heard him say,

'Will you take your clothes off?' and felt a moment's panic, for under the bright rays of the sun where was there to hide?

I don't have to hide anything with Seth, she thought. I want him to know me as I am.

She kicked off her sneakers and socks, drew her jeans down her legs and pulled her pink shirt over her head. Seth let his jeans drop to the sand. As she slowly took off her underwear, her eyes were full of shyness and uncertainty.

'You're so beautiful,' he said huskily, and almost tentatively traced the arc of her ribs and the concavity of her belly. 'So fragile ... so finely made.'

She gazed at him dumbly, her throat bursting with questions. Are you sure this is right? she wanted to cry. Are you still afraid of me? Do you love me?

He looked up, saw the trouble in her face and said fiercely, 'Don't talk, Tascha—not now. This is a time for love, not words.'

And because she wanted to believe him, Tascha let the questions drop to the back of her mind. She stood quietly while he lifted strands of her hair to cover her shoulders and breasts, and felt an inner trembling begin because of the intensity in his face. He kissed her mouth, then kissed her hair and the whiteness of her skin through the hair; and all the while she stood, letting the trembling gather.

Then Seth moved away from her, spreading his shirt and her jacket on the grass, which was starred with the violet-blue of speedwell and the polished yellow of buttercups. He took her by the hand and led her to this makeshift bed, where they lay down side by side. He pressed his head between her breasts; his tongue found her nipples.

Tascha had never made love before. Because she could not depend on experience as a guide, she had to fall back

on her intuition and sensitivity and, because she loved
Seth, her unbounded generosity. The innocence of her
first caresses was also immensely provocative, and Seth
made no secret of his desire. She discovered the tautness
of his belly, the rounded smoothness of his shoulders,
the strength of his legs wrapped around her own, and
all the mystery and power of his manhood. And she discovered in herself a woman she had scarcely known
existed, a woman of passionate hungers and needs, who
was increasingly unafraid to make those needs known.

They started making love as if it were a leisurely dance
whose steps they had somehow always known. But the
tempo of music increased and the rhythms became wild
and pagan. Their hunger for each other was un-
ashamed, their kisses avid: teeth nibbled lips; tongues
danced. Tascha's breasts were crushed against Seth's
chest, for he had clasped her by the hips. She opened
to the slow, tumescent movements of his body against
hers and threw back her head, her eyes closed, the sun
burning her lids. When his fingers found the moist, pet-
alled flesh between her legs, her whole body shuddered
in response, for it was a touch that reached to her very
core. She opened eyes dazzled with wonder and looked
straight into his, beginning to understand the power of
love to unite and make one.

He guided her hand to hold him when he was both
most sensitive and most vulnerable. But, as he began to
enter her, her tiny indrawn breath was of pain, not
pleasure. He stopped, and said in sudden consternation,
'Tascha, have you never——'

She put her fingers to his lips and gave him back his
own request. 'This is a time for love, not words,' she
said, and kissed him with all the love that was in her
heart.

He held her close, his breath warm on her cheek. 'I
had no idea,' he said. 'I'll be gentle, Tascha, I promise.'

As though he were wooing her all over again, and as
though he had all the time in the world to win her, Seth
caressed her with hands and mouth, slowly, sensuously,
until her heart was racing in her breast and her body
was on fire with wanting him. This time, the pain was
only fleeting when his body joined with hers; the pleasure
was exquisite. She felt herself losing control, being taken
over by the rhythms that throbbed like ancient music in
her veins, until she was deaf to all but their insistent
notes and blind to everything but the brilliance of the
sun. And then she became them: the sun, the crystal-
clear water, the soaring of the eagle, the yellow heart of
the flower; and none of them was herself and all of them
were Seth. When she cried out his name, her voice
sobbing like a waterfall, she felt him break within her
and saw under her closed lids all the myriad hues of the
rainbow.

For a long time Tascha lay still in Seth's arms, and
again it was as if words were unnecessary, for they had
said all there was to say with their bodies. The sun
resumed its rightful place in the sky; the eagle had long
ago vanished. Tascha became conscious of sand against
her back and of the weight of Seth's sweat-slicked body.
She felt immeasurably different from the woman of half
an hour ago, for she now knew what belonging truly
meant. She would always belong to Seth, she thought
drowsily. But, paradoxically, she belonged more truly to
herself than she ever had before.

Seth levered himself up on one elbow, his gaze wandering over her love-flushed cheeks and soft mouth. 'I
hope I didn't hurt you,' he murmured.

'Not at all.' She gave a tiny, incredulous laugh. 'I feel
wonderful!'

'So do I . . .' He glanced around at the green-edged
lake. 'You *are* the woman who belongs here, Tascha.'

It was not a declaration of love, but it was not a lightly spoken statement, either; and Seth had given himself fully and generously to the act of love. Tascha gave him a quick, hard hug and said apologetically, 'A rock seems to have imbedded itself in my right hip.'

Seth stood up, pulling her with him. He brushed at her shoulder. 'You've got sand all over you—why don't we go for a swim?'

She eyed the mirror-like surface of the lake distrustfully. 'I bet the water's cold.'

'If I can get in, you can.' He puffed up his chest. 'Or are you admitting I'm superior to you?'

She also mistrusted the gleam in his eye. She grabbed his hand and said, 'We'll go together.'

They ran down the slope into the water. Tascha shrieked out loud as the lake's ice-cold hands clamped around her ankles, then grabbed at her knees. She flopped forwards and vengefully splashed Seth as hard and as fast as she could. He was laughing at her through the spray, his teeth gleaming, water running in rivulets down his big body, and for a moment her hand stilled. He is Adam to my Eve, she thought in wonderment, the man I love more than I can say.

'Are you OK?' he yelled.

She thrust her face into the water and did a dozen crawl strokes that were distinguished by vigour rather than style, and then ran for the shore, Seth at her heels. Shivering on the land, her flesh covered by goose-bumps, she wailed, 'We haven't got a towel!'

'I've got one in the haversack—if you're nice to me, I'll share it with you.'

Her eyes twinkling, Tascha ordered, 'Get the towel, Seth, before I freeze to death.'

By the time she had scrubbed herself dry and hauled on her clothes, the warmth of the sun had begun to penetrate her chilled skin. She felt tinglingly alive and very happy. 'I deserve half an hour in the sauna tonight after that ordeal,' she grumbled, rubbing at the wet ends of her hair.

'So you didn't like my lovemaking?'

She chuckled. 'You know I didn't mean that.'

He was suddenly serious. '*Did* you like it, Tascha?'

She padded across the sand in her bare feet and linked her arms around his waist. 'I loved every moment of it,' she said.

Had he wanted to, Seth could have said, I love you; it would have been the logical moment. Instead he said, 'Give me the towel and I'll dry your hair.'

Tascha was glad that the towel hid her face, for his silence had tarnished her happiness. Seth was afraid of love, she knew that. She would be very naïve to equate the sexual act, no matter how passionate or how generous, with love.

When her hair was as dry as the towel could make it, she ran her fingers through it and pulled it back into a ponytail again. 'You'd better get going,' she said casually.

He glanced up at the sun. 'I'm going to walk you back to the jeep, Tascha. Then you can drive to the lodge and come back for me around four.'

'I can remember the way,' she protested. 'Pretty hard to get lost around here.'

'I spotted the male grizzly between here and the lodge early this morning, around five. It looked as though he was headed the opposite way—but I'd just as soon go with you, to be sure.'

Tascha did not argue. As they set off towards the rocky rim of the plain, she asked, 'What should I do if I ever come face to face with a grizzly, Seth? Besides trying to stave off a heart attack, that is.'

He seemed glad to talk about something so impersonal. 'The worst thing you can do is startle a bear. So it's a good idea to make a fair bit of noise when you're hiking. Sing, whistle, carry a couple of tin cups that rattle against each other, anything to warn the bear of your approach and give him time to get away. Because nine times out of ten he'll have no more desire to meet you than you have to meet him.'

'And what about the tenth time?'

'If he's standing watching you, then back off, slowly. No sudden movements, nothing to alarm him. If he should start to follow you, then move faster. But a bear can outrun you easily... so you might have to stand and face him and wave your arms and make lots of noise. If that doesn't discourage him,' Seth finished with a touch of grimness, 'play dead and pray.'

'Have you ever been chased by one?'

'Sure have. Got between a sow and her cubs once—text-book case of what not to do. Luckily, I wasn't far from the jeep and I got to it before she got to me.' He looked down at his companion. 'But I don't want to scare you unnecessarily, Tascha. The bear population's fairly sparse up here, and the odds of running into trouble are small.'

He began telling her of some of his adventures with animals over the years, and in no time they had reached the jeep. Seth pulled the keys out of his jacket pocket. 'Stay between the ditches,' he said lightly.

'I don't have my licence with me.'

'I doubt if you'll meet a policeman.'

She took the keys, being careful not to touch him, for he no longer seemed like the man with whom she had exchanged such incredible intimacies. 'I'll see you at four,' she said in a low voice.

'I'll do the best I can for you.'

For a moment, Tascha did not know what he meant; Andrei Belov seemed very remote compared to the man at her side. 'Oh,' she stammered, 'thank you. I know you will.'

He kissed her quickly on the lips and gave her shoulder a little squeeze. 'You shouldn't need the four-wheel drive. Just use the gears as you would any normal vehicle.'

She watched him stride away; his loose-limbed gait covered the ground very efficiently. The impetuous, fiery part of her temperament wanted to shout after him that she did not give a damn about the four-wheel drive, that she wanted to be told she was loved. But Tascha had grown up with Olga, and consequently understood patience. She climbed in the jeep, started up the engine and racketed up the slope.

CHAPTER TEN

TASCHA was back at the riverbed at a little before four, and immediately spotted Seth across the rocks several hundred yards from her. Now that she was about to hear the verdict, she discovered Andrei Belov was not a remote figure at all. If he refused to see her, denying any possibility that she was his daughter, she was thrown back on Olga, who had hated her, and on a father who had not cared enough about her even to have left his name. She slid over into the passenger seat and waited, her throat tight.

But, as Seth steadily closed the distance between them, she realised something else. No matter what the verdict, she was infinitely the richer for her brief stay on the tundra. She had discovered a land whose vastness and majesty spoke to her spirit. But, far more important, she had discovered love. She loved Seth deeply and without reserve, and in some indefinable way that love had made her appreciate her own sense of identity, her own worth. It would tear her apart if she had to leave here without Seth; but it would, she thought soberly, be better to have loved and lost than never to have loved at all.

Seth climbed into the driver's seat and threw the empty backpack on to the tarpaulin. Then he turned to face Tascha.

'He'll see you,' he said evenly. 'His wife Marya died in Russia. Marya had blonde hair and blue eyes. Andrei escaped with his daughter, whose name was Natascha, and the family housekeeper, Olga Denisov. He left Olga in Montreal with the child while he came west looking for a place to live. Olga wrote to him of the child's death. Olga did not have a child of her own.'

Tascha stared down at her hands. 'When can I see him?' she whispered.

'I'll take you there after dinner tonight.' Seth started up the jeep.

Something was wrong...something in Seth's voice. 'Aren't you glad for me?'

He eased the jeep into gear and began driving towards the road. 'It's funny,' he said, 'had you asked me before if I thought you were Andrei's daughter, I would have said no. Such things don't happen in real life. The Anastasias are all frauds...But it would seem I was wrong.'

'Don't you want me to be his daughter?'

'Of course I do. It gives you an identity, a family background, a history.'

'Then what's the problem?' she persisted anxiously.

Seth wrestled with the wheel as he hit a rut in the road. 'Had I thought you were Andrei's daughter, I would never have made love to you.'

It is better to have loved and lost...the words echoed mockingly in Tascha's brain. 'Why ever not?' she blurted.

'It's obvious, I would have thought,' he said impatiently. 'My father was Andrei's first friend in this country, and I've known Andrei for twenty years. Despite the difference in age between us, we also are friends, and I've always considered myself honoured to be one of the few people he trusts...his experiences in Russia left him secretive, almost paranoid, so he doesn't trust easily. Then you turn up, and it would now seem you are his daughter—so what do I do? I seduce you! I seduce the virginal daughter of the man who trusts me.' His voice was heavy with self-contempt. 'Great behaviour!

Wonderful behaviour! Just tell me one thing—how am I going to explain it to Andrei?'

'You don't have to!' Tascha said furiously. 'You're talking in clichés. And you're talking as if I had no part in the seduction whatsoever. I wanted you, Seth, and I'm the one who knew I was a virgin—are you forgetting that?'

'I should never have done it,' he said tightly, and she realised she might just as well not have spoken. She sat in a frustrated silence, until slowly, like ice creeping over the surface of a pond, she began to understand all the implications of Seth's speech. He had seduced her: a sentence that reduced that glorious union by the silver lake to something that could have happened in a cheap hotel room. Something sordid. Certainly, it could not have meant to Seth what it had meant to her: an inevitable step in the progression of love. She loved Seth. She had made love to him freely and happily. She wanted to marry him, to be with him for ever. Whereas he was worrying about seduction!

She said in a cold voice, 'You may be sure I shall never tell your friend Andrei what happened today. As you and I are both consenting adults, I don't consider it any of his business.'

'I disagree with you,' Seth said in an even colder voice. 'I've abused his friendship. I'll have to tell him.' They then sat side by side in an icy silence until the jeep pulled up beside the woodshed at the lodge. 'We'll go as soon after dinner as possible,' Seth said. 'I'll leave you there overnight and come back for you first thing in the morning—I don't want the guests asking too many questions.'

Not trusting herself to speak, Tascha got out of the jeep and went straight to the kitchen, where Mae was peeling potatoes. Mae took one look at her face. 'Not much use asking you what kind of day you had,' she said.

'Don't ask or I'll cry in the soup,' Tascha rejoined with a shaky smile. 'What are we having tonight, Mae?'

To produce dinner for sixteen people seemed marvellously simple after all the emotional upheavals of the day. Afterwards, Tascha ate as quickly as she could, helped Mae clean up, then ran to her tent, where she changed into clean jeans and her long-sleeved blue shirt. She brushed her hair into a knot on her head, put on perfume and a little lipstick and stared at her reflection in her hand-mirror. What would he think of her, this reclusive man who wrote books that were frighteningly intelligent and full of wisdom? Would he know her for his daughter through the pull of blood, and embrace her as his own? Or would he be polite and doubtful and distant?

'Hurry up, Tascha!' Seth called from outside the tent.

She made a face at herself in the mirror, and went out to meet him; but no one could have been as polite and distant as Seth on the drive to the riverbed and the hike up the valley. They passed to one side of the lake, which the westering sun had tinted an opalescent pink. Tascha looked away, stumbling a little in the grass, and fastened her eyes on Seth's hiking boots.

Fifteen minutes past the lake, they came to a creek. Seth crossed it, leading Tascha towards a bluff and a cluster of poplars and birch that had grown taller than most; a path led through them into a clearing in which stood a small sturdily built wooden cabin with a metal chimney, from which drifted a thin wreath of blue smoke.

Tascha stopped at the edge of the clearing, her legs suddenly refusing to carry her forwards. The clearing in the fading light was full of sinister shadows, and the man who lived in this cabin would be the ogre of all the fairy stories she had read as a child. Struck with terror, she stood rooted to the spot.

Seth said quietly, 'Tascha, everything will be all right—you'll see.'

His smile was that of the man who had made love to her. She clutched his sleeve unashamedly and forced her legs to move. Seth called, 'Andrei? We're here,' his voice sounding unnaturally loud in the clearing.

From their left someone called back, 'Coming!' The poplar leaves rustled against each other, and a man's figure emerged into the clearing. He was carrying a pail of water.

Tascha let go of Seth's sleeve and stepped forwards, and in the dim light her fair hair was like an aureole around her face and her blue eyes looked very dark.

The bucket dropped to the ground, its handle clanking against the side. The water sloshed over the man's feet. But he did not even look down. His eyes glued to Tascha's face, he whispered, 'Marya! My God... Marya!'

As clumsily as a child taking its first step, he moved towards her, his arms outstretched. Then, so suddenly that she jumped, his hands thrust her away in repudiation and his face twisted with agony. 'Marya's dead,' he muttered. 'Dead... you can't be Marya!' He turned and ran from the clearing, crashing through the bushes like a terrified animal.

Tascha had taken one instinctive step after him. Then she stopped and looked back at Seth, her face aghast. Almost sobbing, she cried, 'Oh, Seth, he ran away from me! What will I do? Should I go after him?'

'No—wait. He'll come back, I'm sure.'

'Why did he run away?'

Seth grasped her shoulders. 'Don't you understand, Tascha? You look so much like Marya that he thought you *were* Marya—she *must* have been your mother.'

Tascha's shoulders sagged; she felt none of the elation she had anticipated. 'I suppose she must have been... but, Seth, will he always look at me and see her?'

Seth shook her. 'He'll see you for yourself!'

She leaned against his chest and let him enfold her in his arms and felt some of her confusion subside, usurped by the clarity of her love for Seth. Then she heard, from behind her, the rustle of leaves and the snap of twigs. Slowly, she straightened.

Andrei Belov stepped back into the clearing. He walked up to Tascha, took her hands and said quietly, 'You must forgive me, my dear. It is twenty-one years since I have seen Marya, and you are very like her... welcome, Natascha.' He leaned forward and kissed her formally on both cheeks, then added, 'Let's go inside—I want to have a good look at you. Seth, perhaps you could fill the bucket I so unceremoniously emptied, and we will make coffee.'

He took Tascha's hand and led her into the cabin, where he lit the oil lamp on the shelf. In its steady glow, he scrutinised Tascha's features, and as he did so she had her first good look at him. He was not much taller than she, a wiry man with the weathered skin of one who loves the outdoors. His hair was tidily combed and his grey beard neatly trimmed. But his eyes caught and held her attention. They, too, were grey and, as Seth had once said to her, they looked as though they had forgotten nothing he had ever seen. She was touched to the heart when she saw they were covered with a sheen of tears. 'So, daughter,' he said unsteadily, 'after all these years, we meet again.' Then he folded her in his arms and held her close. She hugged him back and let her own tears flow.'

The cabin door squeaked open and Seth came in, carrying the pail. Gently, Andrei released Tascha. 'We will make the coffee before you go, Seth.'

Seth said expressionlessly, 'I think I'll leave right away, Andrei.' He looked the older man straight in the eye. 'But I have one question for you. Why did you never tell me about Marya and the child?'

'Your father knew—but your father kept everything I said in confidence. And, by the time you were old enough to understand, I no longer needed to talk about them. Besides, I had no photographs of Marya and the child to show you, nothing concrete to remember them by. Only memories, and those, of course, I deal with in my books.'

Seth's expression gave nothing away. 'I see. Well, I'd better be going. I'll be back tomorrow around ten or eleven, Tascha—if anyone at the lodge asks after you, I'll say you've got the morning off.'

Andrei interposed quietly, 'I'll walk Natascha to the road tomorrow. Why don't you get there around ten-thirty?'

For a moment, something flared in Seth's eyes, an emotion Tascha could not have called friendly. 'Ten-thirty,' he said in a clipped voice, and turned to go.

Tascha could not bear for him to leave her so precipitately. 'I'll see you on your way,' she offered.

'There's no need.'

'Please, Seth.' She followed him out of the door and across the clearing.

He stopped at the edge of the poplars, and his eyes were blacker than the shadowed trees. 'I'm glad you've found your father, Tascha—and your mother,' he said.

It had been an effort for him to speak. Hurt without knowing why, Tascha answered, 'I still can't quite take it in.'

Seth added harshly, 'Andrei's like my father—I never realised that before. He loved Marya so much that twenty years later her image is still as clear to him as the day she died. That's why he never spoke of her—I know it!'

'If he hadn't loved her, I wouldn't exist,' Tascha protested, smiling a little.

'The cost's too high,' Seth grated. 'We're fed this image of love as something charming and sweet, like decorated chocolates in a heart-shaped box. Love isn't like that at all—it's the most destructive emotion there is.'

'I can't believe that, Seth,' she said vehemently. 'Don't tell me that what we did on the lakeshore was destructive. It was beautiful and intimate—and full of love, damn it!'

'You're not the first woman to equate sex with love.'

Tascha drew back, her breath escaping in a hiss of pain. 'So, in gaining a father, am I losing you?' she asked in a voice she scarcely recognised as her own.

'Oh, God—I don't know!' Like a man possessed, Seth buried his face in her neck, holding her so tightly she could hardly breathe. 'I can still see my father's face the day my mother died...he looked like a man in hell, Tascha. And that's what love has meant to me ever since.' As he let her go, she staggered. 'You must get back to Andrei. I'll see you tomorrow.'

Before she could think of any reply, the trees swallowed him in their shadows. Trying to school her mind to blankness, Tascha went back to the cabin, which was redolent with the odour of the coffee percolating on a spirit stove. She said, striving for normality, 'That smells good.'

Andrei smiled, a smile that robbed his words of any possible offence. 'You're in love with Seth.'

Her jaw dropped. She gazed into the all-seeing grey eyes, knew denial was futile, and said with assumed calm, 'Yes.'

'And he with you, I would suspect.'

'You suspect wrong,' she answered vigorously.

'I've known Seth a long time. I've never seen him behave the way he has the last couple of days.'

Tascha sat down in an old-fashioned rocking-chair and realised that she could say whatever she liked to this bearded man who was, incredibly, her father. 'You don't play around with small talk, do you?'

'Never.'

'A waste of time.'

They exchanged a look of perfect understanding. 'Do you know how I feel?' Tascha said impulsively. 'Free! Liberated...as though I can tell you anything and everything under the sun. You'll listen and understand and never be shocked.' Her smile was wry. 'Very different from Olga.'

'We will talk about Olga later...but now, Seth. Seth is afraid of love, Natascha, and with good reason. Catherine, his mother, died two years after I met Neil, so I had plenty of time to observe that marriage. She was jealous of our friendship, you know, so he never really became my friend until after she died. Ah, I suppose the poets would have called it a great love, what was between them. Certainly they themselves did.'

'But you didn't.'

'No. Love is generous, Natascha. It looks beyond itself and the more it gives of itself, the more it has to give. Catherine and Neil Curtis were the most selfish couple I have ever met.'

Strong words, thought Tascha, and knew with a strange excitement that Andrei was giving her the key to understanding Seth. 'Where did Seth fit into that marriage?'

'Clever girl—he didn't, of course. He had a beautiful mother and a handsome father, who gave him bicycles and ponies and sent him to boarding-school in the winter and to camp in the summer. But they did not give him time. They did not give him love—they had none to give, being so enraptured with each other. It's no wonder Neil was devastated when Catherine died. He had no other resources to fall back on. So Seth grew up on the fringe of what was touted as a great love affair, and learned that love is cruel and self-centred, and that the end of love is an all-absorbing grief. No wonder he is frightened of falling in love!'

There had been passion in Andrei's voice. Thoughtfully, Tascha watched him pour the coffee into two pottery mugs. 'Seth and I made love today,' she said evenly. 'For the first time—and perhaps the last.'

Andrei passed her the sugar; he did not look at all shocked. 'Seth is not a man to make love lightly... so the situation is moving towards a crisis for him. I know he's capable of love, Natascha, for I have seen him with injured animals and watched him play with the children of the miners.'

The first time she had seen Seth he had been involved in a labour of love, Tascha remembered, saving an Indian boy from arrest. Trying to remember all the details, she recounted the story to Andrei.

He nodded, unsurprised. 'But he has never given love to a woman. I've been waiting for the right one to come along—not expecting her to be my own daughter!' He raised his coffee to her in ironic salute.

'Do you mind?'

'I would be delighted. He's a fine man.'

'I'm afraid I'm going to lose him,' Tascha said honestly.

Andrei paused, then said calmly, 'I know very little of your present life, but I would be very happy if in the autumn you chose to move to Vancouver. I own a house on a secluded cove outside the city—you could live with me if you wished, or live in the city and stay on weekends.' Another of those little salutes with the mug. 'Seth's house is only a mile from mine.'

In silence, Tascha looked at this man who was her father, knowing he was offering her a home; more than that, he was offering to share his much-valued privacy. 'Am I greedy to want both of you?' she asked. 'You, and Seth as well?'

'Only human.'

'I hate Montreal!' she exclaimed, suddenly discovering that was true.

'So... tell me about yourself and Olga.'

Tascha did the best she could, being scrupulously fair, for she knew she had not always been the easiest child to raise; but the picture she painted was a grim one and Andrei was capable of picking up what she did not say. She finished by telling him how guilty she had always felt for her inability to love Olga, and how happy she was to be absolved of that guilt. Then she said hesitantly, 'Seth has helped me to understand, though, that I owe Olga something. She was a survivor, you see, a hard worker who wouldn't take charity from anyone—she never spent the money you gave her twenty years ago, for instance. Because of her, I've learned to be independent, to stand on my own two feet and work for what I've wanted.'

'Not bad lessons.'

'Not bad at all.' In a low voice, Tascha added, 'But I've never understood why she hated me.'

'I can explain that.' Andrei stared into his coffee, his eyes bleak. 'Olga was a distant cousin of Marya's, very poor and with no family. So we took her on as a housekeeper. A charitable act, no doubt, but not one for which we were blessed. Olga was not beautiful or charming or clever like her cousin, nor did she have a husband and child. She was, I think, bitterly envious of Marya, although she kept it well hidden. After Marya died—she caught pneumonia our last winter in exile, we had no money for drugs or proper foods, it was a terrible time...'

For a moment, he was lost in memory. 'Well,' he went on heavily, 'after Marya died, I believed Olga thought I would turn to her for comfort, perhaps even marry her—that became clear on our voyage to this new land. I discouraged her—kindly enough, I thought—and told her once I was settled in the west I would hire a nanny for you, because it did not seem fair she should have to look after Marya's child. I was younger then, and not very wise. Olga must have brooded over that rejection, and her actions were, I suppose, a way of punishing me. She wrote to me saying you had died. My last tie to Marya, gone—you can imagine how I felt. And she would have hated you, Natascha, because you are very like Marya. Her only satisfaction must have been to deprive you of all the benefits of being my daughter and to watch you grow up without them.'

Tascha shivered, remembering Seth's words. 'The destructive side of love,' she whispered.

As if he had read her mind, Andrei said sharply, 'Don't compare Olga and Seth! Olga was truly incapable of love. Even self-love. But Seth has a big soul. If Seth could free himself of the past, you would be loved as few women are.'

'A big soul,' Tascha repeated softly, liking the phrase. 'But how to free him, Andrei?' Then she flushed and mumbled apologetically, 'I'm sorry, I should call you Father, but I—I'm not quite used to the idea yet.'

Andrei said easily, 'You will call me Father when it seems natural. And Seth will admit he loves you when the time is right.' When Tascha gave a huge sigh, he laughed. 'You have inherited all Marya's impatience, I see!'

As darkness crept over the land, he told her more about Marya, about his life in Russia and about his work, and drew her out to talk more fully about herself. They drained the coffee-pot and made more; they ate oatmeal biscuits and cheese at one o'clock in the morning; when the first pale light of dawn appeared, they went for a walk along the banks of the creek so Andrei could show her a red fox den; and all the time they talked. But at six o'clock, when Tascha started yawning, great yawns that she could not hide, Andrei pulled out a spare sleeping-bag and she curled up in it and slept.

They left the cabin at ten to walk to the road, and it seemed only natural and right to Tascha that the sun be shining in a cloudless sky and that they see a herd of caribou traversing the ridge where the poppies grew. The jeep was parked at the riverbed. Seth and Andrei exchanged a few words, then Seth said, with the abruptness Tascha was beginning to expect, 'We'd better go, Tascha, I have to take a couple of the guests to the creek again to photograph the flowers.'

She nodded, then turned to Andrei. Without warning, her eyes filled with tears. She said incoherently, 'You have no idea how happy I am that I've found you and that you're my father and that now I know who my mother really was. You've been so open with me—I feel as though I've known you for a very long time.'

He put his arms around her, kissed her on both cheeks and said warmly, 'I also am more happy than I can say. Goodbye, Natascha. I'll hike up to the lodge on Sunday, while the guests are gone, to see you again.'

She hugged him convulsively. 'Goodbye, Father,' she said, and climbed quickly into the jeep. Tears were pouring down her face as Seth drove away, but through them she saw the thin figure of her father tramping steadily across the rocks to re-enter the isolated world that was his home.

She closed her eyes and leaned back against the seat, and despite the rough road she fell asleep on the way to the lodge. When the jeep heeled sideways approaching the gate, her head banged against Seth's shoulder. She woke with a start, tried to lift her head and cried out with pain at the sudden pull to her scalp. Seth braked to a halt. 'Hold on,' he ordered. 'Your hair's caught in a button on my shirt.'

She winced as his fingers untangled her hair. 'There,' he said curtly. 'It's free.'

His profile was as rigid as granite. Not stopping to think, Tascha rested her hand on his forearm and said, 'My father told me quite a bit about your parents, Seth...it helped me to understand why you're so afraid of love.'

With a deliberation that was an insult in itself, Seth removed her hand from his arm and dropped it back in her lap. 'I'm not asking to be understood. If any of the guests want to know where you've been, you hiked out to the creek this morning and I agreed to bring you back.'

His rebuff was like a slap in the face. Her eyes flashed much as Marya's might have done a quarter of a century ago, and as the jeep began creeping towards the gate she announced, 'You'd better get used to the idea of having me around. Andrei has asked me to live with him this winter.'

'You'll have him—you won't need me.'

She remembered the little boy who had never stepped inside the golden circle of his parents' love, and said passionately, 'Love isn't like that, Seth! The more one gives away, the more one has to give.'

'Since when have you become such an expert?' he snarled. 'Don't preach to me, Tascha, and don't tell me what I should be feeling!'

'I'm only trying to help!'

'I don't need or want your help.'

'Fine,' Tascha said furiously. 'It must be great to be omnipotent! You can let me out here—I'm damned if I want to spent one more second in your company than I have to.'

He slammed on the brakes again. She said meanly, 'I hope all the guests are lined up behind the telescopes, watching us. You can tell them from me that you're as bad-tempered as a grizzly and as mean as a wolverine. Good*bye*!' And she slammed the door every bit as hard as he had applied the brakes.

Rocks flying from the tyres, the jeep started up the hill again. From the shrubbery beside the fence, Jasmine said appreciatively, 'Boy, did you tell him off!'

Tascha jumped. Clutching at her dignity, her cheeks scarlet, she said, 'It was a private disagreement.'

'Yeah?' Jasmine eyed her shrewdly. 'You look as though you were up all night.'

Very much aware of her crumpled clothes and the circles under her eyes, Tascha replied, 'If I was, it was not for any of the reasons that you might think.'

Jasmine sighed. 'He's sure a lot more interested in you than in me. Being a virgin didn't seem to do me much good.'

It was not the time to recall her own lost virginity. Tascha said in a stifled voice, 'I hope you'll enjoy your hike today, Jasmine.'

'I'm not going.' Sulkily, Jasmine kicked at a clump of earth. 'I'm sick of the boring old tundra. The flowers are so little, you step on them before you see them, and once you've seen one caribou you've seen them all.'

There was genuine misery underlying Jasmine's drooping, heavily carmined lower lip, nor could Tascha be so wrapped up in her own troubles as to ignore it. 'You're a city person, Jasmine. There's nothing wrong with that.'

'The batteries even wore out on my ghetto blaster.'

The ultimate tragedy, Tascha thought drily. 'Think how much you'll appreciate civilisation when you get back to it.'

'I'm going to get my hair dyed, buy a whole lot of new clothes and order a twelve-inch pizza all for myself,' said Jasmine, looking marginally less doleful.

Tascha laughed. 'With pepperoni, onions, green pepper, double cheese and pineapple!'

'You forgot the mushrooms.'

Tascha said impetuously, 'Why don't we go for a walk together after dinner, Jasmine? You could tell me more about yourself.'

'OK,' said Jasmine. 'We'll show Seth we can do without him, right?'

'Right,' Tascha replied, wishing it were so.

She slept through the lunch hour, washed some clothes, helped Mae with dinner and went for a walk with Jasmine. Many of Jasmine's opinions were formed by the pop culture of her peers, and her sexual mores were shaky, to say the least, but beneath her brash talk Tascha could discern confusion and loneliness. Jasmine's mother was on husband number two since Clyde, and affair number six or seven; her method of bringing up her daughter seemed to be to lavish her with money and ignore her.

It was nearly ten o'clock when they rambled up the driveway towards the lodge. Clyde waved to them from the balcony. 'You missed two gyrfalcons!' he cried.

'Gee,' said Jasmine, 'how about that?'

Tascha smothered a laugh. 'I'm going up to see if there are any caribou out on the barrens,' she said. 'Goodnight, Jasmine. I enjoyed our walk.'

'Me, too. See you.' Jasmine blew an expert bubble with her gum and sauntered off to the cabin she shared with her father.

Clyde and Martin were the only occupants of the lodge. Clyde showed her a solitary bull caribou far out on the tundra, and said, as she was peering through the telescope, 'That was nice of you to go for a walk with Jasmine.'

'I enjoyed her company,' Tascha said absently, watching the dip and sway of the antlers as the animal grazed.

'She needs more female company. Older women, that is,' Clyde said, then stuttered, 'I didn't mean you were old, Tascha, I meant older than Jasmine.'

She took pity on him, glancing up from the telescope to say, 'We had a nice talk—she told me quite a bit about herself. Mind you, I think she's just about ready to head for the bright lights of Toronto.'

Clyde sighed. 'Once we're home, she goes back to her mother.'

On the far side of the room, Martin seemed to be absorbed in his book. 'Maybe she should live with you,' Tascha suggested.

'But I've never remarried, and I think she'd need a woman's touch.'

His words called to mind lace doilies and frilly curtains. 'Nonsense!' said Tascha bracingly. 'Lots of single men are bringing up their children these days.'

With rare humour, Clyde said, 'I think she'd be bringing me up, not the reverse.'

Unfortunately, Tascha was inclined to agree. She swallowed a yawn. 'I've got to turn in, Clyde, I'm tired. See you tomorrow.'

He was studying her as if he had never seen her before. She gave him a quick smile, hoping he was not getting any ideas, and ran downstairs. Not even the memory of her fight with Seth could keep her awake that night; and at six-fifteen the next morning, when Seth came looking for her, she was still fast asleep.

Seth called her name outside the tent, but that merely fitted into a dream Tascha was having, and a little smile flitted across her lips. He pushed aside the tent flap and went in, stooped low. She was lying on her back, her hair spread on the pillow, one bare arm flung over her head. The only sound in the tent was the quiet rhythm of her breathing.

For at least five minutes Seth stayed where he was, hunkered down by the metal cot, watching the sleeping woman. No one could have guessed his exact thoughts, although Tascha certainly would have known they were not happy.

Muffled by the canvas walls of the tent came the lonely cry of a golden plover. Seth stirred, gave his head a little shake and said in a loud, flat voice, 'Tascha, it's time to wake up. Tascha!'

She turned her head, rubbed her eyes, and murmured in confusion, 'Seth . . . is anything wrong?'

'It's time to get up,' he repeated in the same expressionless voice.

She stated the obvious. 'I was sound asleep . . . I didn't get much sleep last night.' And, because she was still not quite awake and none of her guards were up, she smiled at Seth and said naïvely, 'How nice when you're the first person I see in the morning.'

A spasm crossed his face. 'Mae will be waiting for you.'

'Seth,' she said softly, 'kiss me good morning.'

Her eyes were as clear as the water in the lake and her sleep-warm lips were a gentle curve. His face tightened. 'Tascha, if I kiss you good morning, Mae will be waiting a long time.'

'No, she won't. Just one kiss, because we let the sun go down on our anger and we shouldn't have done that.'

'You make things too simple, Tascha.'

'You make things too complicated. Just a kiss.' She opened her arms to him.

Seth knelt by the side of the bed and awkwardly took her in his arms. She rested her hands on his shoulders, feeling the tension in them, and lifted her face, kissing him with love and generosity and not a trace of sensuality. Then she eased back on the pillow, holding him away from her, and said, 'No fights today?'

In a voice so low she had to strain to hear it, Seth said, 'You tear me apart.'

'I don't mean to!' she answered in quick distress.

He straightened, increasing the distance between them, and said with a lightness that was almost successful, 'Well, we won't argue about it—no fights, remember?'

Tascha wanted to say, I love you. But she also wanted to make him smile. 'So I have to get my mind on Mae and the muffins, hmm? Very difficult when you're around.'

His smile reached his eyes this time. 'Flattered, I'm sure. Get up, Tascha—or I'll enlist the aid of the cold water that's outside your tent.'

She sat up in a hurry, her breasts bouncing under her knit nightgown. 'You wouldn't!'

He looked at her breasts, said wryly, 'I'll dump it on myself, instead,' and backed out of the tent.

She called out, 'We could argue about who needs it most!' and got up, feeling light-headed with love. Maybe Andrei was right, and in time Seth would come to understand that love could bring happiness and fulfilment rather than exclusion and pain. At least they had agreed not to fight, she thought, humming to herself as she got dressed. That was a step in the right direction.

She did not know then that their agreement was to last less than twelve hours, or perhaps she would not have been singing as she mixed the muffin dough and measured out the water for the oatmeal. Her choice of song was quite unconscious. 'I'm in love with a wonderful guy,' she warbled, and Mae, asking no questions, smiled to herself.

CHAPTER ELEVEN

WHEN Seth took the guests to a valley west of the lodge that morning, to look for a rare alpine azalea, Tascha stayed behind to help Mae with some cleaning, and after lunch went for a walk by herself. On the way back, she met Clyde near his cabin. The trip had been a success for Clyde because he had seen a family of rock ptarmigan and a northern shrike; azaleas obviously did not interest him.

Only paying him partial attention, because she was watching the cloud shadows drift over the hills and thinking about Seth, Tascha felt him suddenly grab her sleeve. She glanced at him, expecting him to announce that a rock ptarmigan was standing three feet behind her. But his binoculars were dangling against his jacket and he was looking at her, not the tundra. Looking at her very peculiarly, she thought with a touch of unease, noticing the flush in his cheeks and the agitation of his breathing. But, before she could say anything, he was off in full spate.

'Jasmine was telling me today what a nice walk she had with you the other evening. She says you're the only person she can talk to——'

'Oh, I'm sure I'm not. Look, Clyde, isn't that a plover?'

But not even a bird could deflect Clyde now. 'I've never known her help in the kitchen before she met you, and she's even putting on less make-up...Tascha, I have more than enough money for the three of us, and my house has been appraised at four hundred thousand, you could decorate it any way you liked——'

'Clyde, please, you mustn't——'

'I know I'm not a young man, but I'd be good to you, and Jasmine could live with us if I were married. It would all work out beautifully.' He paused just long enough to take a deep breath. 'So, will you marry me, Tascha?' he asked, and before she could say a word he seized her as resolutely as if she were a telescope on a tripod, and planted a kiss in the vicinity of her mouth.

Unnerved by a mixture of surprise, compassion and dismay, Tascha felt his mouth find hers on his second attempt. He was stronger than she would have expected, and what his kiss lacked in expertise it made up for in enthusiasm. Moreover, he was obviously interpreting her inertia as consent, and it was this which made her gather her scattered wits and shove at his chest with the palms of her hands. She got her head free long enough to sputter, *'Don't,* Clyde!'

But Clyde had discovered the joys of mastery. He kissed her again, very firmly, so that his binoculars dug into her chest. 'I only just thought of the idea myself,' he said, 'so I realise it'll take you a while to get used to it—we must tell Jasmine right away.' He chortled. 'I'm sure she didn't think I had it in me!'

'Clyde, I can't!' Tascha said desperately.

'Can't what?'

'Can't marry you. I'm sorry,' she added miserably, because he looked so pleased with himself and she hated to puncture his self-esteem.

'I've been too hasty,' Clyde said, only a little deflated. 'I should have waited until tomorrow, but that's our last day. Besides, in the business world, I've always learned to seize opportunities when they come up, and there you were walking near my cabin. Not that I see you as an opportunity,' he floundered, 'you're a very lovely young woman.' He managed a courtly little bow, which Tascha considered quite an achievement under the circumstances.

She said firmly, 'Clyde, you've done all the talking so far. Now it's my turn.'

'I would never expect you to do housework,' he said, undeterred, and looked quite ferocious. 'I've hated seeing you slave away in the kitchen every day.'

But Tascha had rather enjoyed her kitchen duty. 'My turn,' she said forcefully. 'It's very sweet of you to have asked me to marry you, and I'm honoured. But I cannot possibly do it.'

He was regarding her rather as if she were a very junior partner objecting to the president's plan. 'You just need a little more time,' he said kindly. 'You could come back to Toronto with us—and stay in a hotel, of course. We could get to know one another better and spend lots of time with Jasmine.'

'I'm not in love with you,' Tascha said bluntly.

'That would come with time,' said Clyde.

She thought of Seth, and winced inwardly, 'No, it wouldn't,' she replied. 'Because—and I don't want you asking any questions—I'm in love with someone else. Perhaps I should have told you. But I really didn't anticipate that you would propose to me.'

Obviously crestfallen, Clyde said, 'Who?'

'No questions. But I'm not going to get over it, I know I'm not, so I really can't marry you.'

Clyde drew his brows together. 'Is he going to marry you?'

She lost some of her forcefulness. 'I don't know.'

'*I'd* be honoured to marry you.'

Tascha did not want him to start all over again. 'No, Clyde! Look, I have to go, Mae's expecting me.'

He suddenly kissed her again, as greedy as a fledgling after food. 'I shall ask you again tomorrow.'

She pulled free, saying breathlessly, 'You'll be wasting your time,' and ran up the bank between the two nearest guest cabins. She had lied to Clyde; it was too early for Mae to be in the kitchen. But when she rounded the right-hand cabin, her heart sank. Too early for Mae; but not for Seth. He was standing by the kitchen door. Even from a distance, he looked extremely angry.

She darted a look over her shoulder, saw that he would have had a perfect view of Clyde's proposal, and called out brightly, 'I hear you found the azaleas.'

He scowled. 'I'm sure that's not why Clyde was kissing you.'

'Clyde asked me to marry him,' Tascha said straight-forwardly; now that she was closer, rage seemed a more appropriate word than anger for Seth's state.

'You didn't seem to be fighting him off.'

'He took me by surprise.'

In a thoroughly nasty voice, Seth asked, 'So should I be congratulating you?'

'What if I said yes?'

'I might feel compelled to tell Clyde that you and I made love just two days ago, and does he mind if the bride-to-be is a little used?'

Exhilarated by his rage, because at least it indicated strong emotion, Tascha commented, '*You're* not proposing to me. Dog in the manger, Seth?'

'Clyde's old enough to be your father,' Seth said coldly.

'So he is. Also, I'm in love with somebody else, and I have no ambitions to be Jasmine's stepmother.'

'*Who?*'

She stared up into his eyes, where fury glowed like live coals. 'You surely don't have to ask that question.'

'Are you saying you're in love with me?'

She refused to lower her gaze. 'Yes.'

There was an appreciable silence, during which Tascha hoped Mae would have the tact to stay away. Finally, Seth said in a strangled voice, 'Are you telling me the truth, Tascha?'

'Oh, yes.'

'But what about Andrei?'

She went on the attack. 'What about him, Seth? My relationship with him and my relationship with you don't have to be mutually exclusive. I'm sure, as I get to know him and spend more time with him, I'll grow to love him. Which, if anything, will only deepen my love for you.' Seth was still staring at her in a baffled silence. She added, 'And let's suppose by some miracle you and I got married and had children...I would love the children because they would be ours, but I would never stop loving you.'

'How can you be so sure?' he burst out.

'I don't know,' she said honestly. 'I guess I've learned an awful lot about love in a short time.'

'I wish I could believe you,' Seth said in a dull voice, then gave an irritable shrug. 'Hell, what's the use of talking about it?'

'You don't love me?' Tascha asked quietly.

His eyes naked with truth, he said, 'It's as though there's a wall between you and me. The same wall I put up when I was just a kid.'

'Pull it down, Seth.'

'I don't know how.'

'You're the only one who can.'

'I'm not sure I want to.' Then, suddenly, his face changed. 'Hi, Mae,' he said with false heartiness. 'Time for dinner?'

Curses on dinner, thought Tascha roundly and smiled at Mae. Seth turned away, his shoulders slumped and his walk that of a much older man. She knew she should not think ill of the dead but, if Neil Curtis had been standing in front of her right then, she would have given him a piece of her mind.

He did not, of course, appear. Tascha followed Mae into the kitchen and began peeling vegetables with truculent swipes of the knife. She had hoped that telling Seth she loved him would break through the wall; but it had not. She had no other weapon to use. Her fate lay in his hands. How trite that sounded, and how helpless it made her feel! Helpless and unhappy.

She found herself watching Seth covertly throughout dinner, not much comforted by the fact that he did not look happy, either. He left the dining-room as soon as he had finished eating; she was busy grinding coffee beans, so she did not see him leave, nor did she see the jeep hurtle down the driveway. Wrapped up in her own thoughts, she was considering and discarding various plans.

She could go to Seth's cabin and try to seduce him. But Seth would almost certainly reject her.

She could run to Andrei with her problems. However, it was her problem, not Andrei's, and she did not want to begin that relationship on the wrong foot.

She could get lost on the tundra and Seth would find her and be so glad to see her that he would propose. But how could she lose herself on the tundra when there were a dozen guests—minus Jasmine—scanning every ridge and hollow for caribou?

She could fall ill and Seth would nurse her back to health. But she was almost never ill, and doubted she could fake it as easily as Mae.

Tascha began to wash the dishes, and because her mind was not on what she was doing she cracked a glass and cut the heel of her hand. But it was Clyde who stemmed the blood and put on a bandage, because Seth seemed to have disappeared. Clyde plainly enjoyed coming to her rescue. She thanked him sourly, took over drying the dishes while Mae washed, and then clumped out of the kitchen. Her hand hurt.

She marched past her tent and banged on the door of Seth's cabin. No answer. By peering in the window, she ascertained that the cabin was indeed empty. She then walked up to the woodshed. The jeep, which had been parked there all day, was gone.

She felt a moment of stark, unreasoning terror. Seth was gone! He had solved the dilemma in his own way by disappearing. The ground rocked beneath Tascha's feet. Like a film in fast-forward, she had a vision of the days and weeks and months ahead of her, all of them empty of Seth, all meaningless.

She swallowed hard. Seth's gone for a drive, a tiny voice of reason whispered. That's all. No need to panic.

Her hand was throbbing and she felt a little sick, for the black side of love had shown its face to her. To love Seth unrequitedly seemed a monstrous sentence. She was not sure she would be able to live with Andrei if Seth were but a mile down the road...

Tascha went to her tent and read for a while; she dozed for half an hour. Then she put on her jacket and walked back to the woodshed. The jeep had not returned.

It was getting late, the sky softening to the pearl-greys and muted pinks of the slow northern sunset. She walked behind the cabins, past Mae's at the very end, and tramped down the slope that led to the road, staring at the ground, her feet automatically avoiding the rocks and tussocks, her mind just as automatically cataloguing the flowering plants that she recognised. The road was much easier walking. She swung along more energetically, the exercise settling her mind. For several minutes she stopped in a hollow in the road to watch a phalarope bob and spin on the surface of a pond, ripples spreading outwards from it in concentric circles. Ruefully, she thought of Clyde's proposal and Seth's rage, and wished with all her heart that Seth could be beside her now, watching the antics of a small grey and white bird on a swampy pond.

The phalarope erupted from the surface of the water and flew to a pond further from the road, a larger one where Tascha could see two other shorebirds. She decided to follow it.

Half an hour later, having abandoned the phalarope and the two smaller birds, that might or might not have been sandpipers, in favour of a family of willow ptarmigan, Tascha found herself wet to the ankles in a bog, where clumps of brilliant green grass were interspersed with dark brown puddles of very wet mud and clumps of willows. She was not afraid of sinking into the bog never to be heard of again, because Clyde had told her the permafrost was only a foot down; but she was not improving the appearance of her sneakers or her socks, and the ptarmigan seemed to have eluded her.

The sun was impaled on the peak of one of the westerly mountains, its rays making miniature golden suns of the scattered ponds on the barrens. The beauty of the scene made Tascha's heart ache; and she was suddenly aware of her isolation and of the silence pressing on her ears. She pulled one foot free of the mud and the homely squelch of her sock in her wet sneaker was immensely reassuring. Home, she thought. Home and bed. As her feet were already wet, she'd head straight back to the road through the willows. It was not really that far.

Trying to balance on the grass clumps, clutching at the bushes for support, she made noisy progress across the bog. She was soon breathing hard, remembering another of Clyde's pearls of knowledge; that a mile on the tundra is the equivalent of five miles on a city pavement. She stopped to rest a moment, and over the sound of her breathing heard willow twigs snap behind her and the slosh of water.

The hair rose on the back of her neck. Her heart seemed to stop altogether, then began thumping like a pneumatic hammer in her breast. Very slowly, she turned her head.

Seventy feet behind her, a large brown bear was ambling through the willows. A grizzly bear!

In that single instant, the details were indelibly etched on her mind. The rounded, fuzzy ears, like those of a teddy bear she had had as a child. The surprisingly long nose. The great hump between the shoulders. The smooth bunch of muscles under the rough, yellow-brown-fur, and the shambling, powerful walk.

Ankle-deep in cold brown water, her muscles frozen and her throat paralysed, Tascha sent up a frantic prayer that the bear would not see her. She had no idea what she would do if it did.

The bear stopped. Its head swung in her direction, its nose testing the air. Its eyes, she thought numbly, were too close together. Like Eddie's.

Seth's instructions rushed into her brain, all jumbled together. She said out loud, in a voice pitched several notes higher than her normal voice, 'It's all right, I'm heading back to the road. You go your way and I'll go mine, and I'm sorry if I startled you. Seth told me never to startle a bear, but as I didn't know you were there it was a bit difficult not to——' And all the while she was speaking, another Tascha was standing a little apart from her, thinking what nonsense she was talking.

The bear took three steps towards her. She related to it, at the top of her voice, everything Seth had told her to do should she find herself in her present predicament. The bear took a couple more steps in her direction.

She began to back up very slowly, partly because none of her muscles wanted to obey her, partly because she could not see where she was going. Raising her arms in the air, she waved them up and down and told the bear about the phalaropes she had seen and how Clyde had proposed to her and she had turned him down. She was making a fool of herself, she knew, and would have given Olga's entire bank account to have had a dozen people at her back guffawing at the babbling of her tongue. The hair had not subsided on her neck and every instinct in her screamed to forget Seth's advice and to run for her life.

But she held tightly to the echo of Seth's voice in her brain, knowing it was her only protection, and knowing also that she must not run. She backed up a little faster. As her heel slipped on some mud and she crashed sideways into a willow bush, the bear raised its nostrils again to catch her scent.

Whimpering with fear, Tascha scrambled to her feet. The distance between herself and the bear had surely lessened. She could feel the primitive, mindless fear of the hunted gather in her body and fought against it, for if it conquered her she was lost. She began shouting at the top of her lungs, sneaking glances over her shoulder to avoid falling again. Another thirty feet and she would be out of the bog.

She stumbled backwards. The bear followed her at an angle, its too-close eyes watching her every move. The ground became firmer. The willows thinned.

Tascha's entire being had become the need to reach the road, as though the road, man-built, would furnish her with some kind of protection. Beyond that, she dared not think.

Her heels were crushing lichen now, and the twisted brown seed-heads of mountain avens. The bear had reached the edge of the bog. She was breathing in hoarse gasps that hurt her throat, and with a strange kind of detachment wondered what she would do if the bear charged. Lie down and play dead, said Seth's voice. Run, said the fear that held her in its grip.

She began to sing, choosing the melodies that she had chirrupped long ago in the junior high school concerts, when all the students had taken part, regardless of whether they could carry a tune or not; she had not bothered auditioning for the school choir. Her wavering treble, the sick, heavy thump of her heart and the crunch of her steps deafened her to the sound of an engine coming along the road. Her first intimation that she and the bear were no longer alone came from the bear, when it stopped in its tracks and looked back over its shoulder. She had been so intimately bound to its small, dark eyes that she found herself following its gaze. Her voice wobbled and died. Her hands fell to her sides. Seth was striding towards her from tussock to tussock, shouting and waving his arms.

Her blood began to sing in her ears. I can't faint now, she thought fuzzily. I can't! We both have to get out of this alive.

She dropped her chin to her chest and took two or three breaths, filling her lungs as deeply as she could and then emptying them. Seth was almost level with her now. The bear was swinging its head from side to side.

Seth said urgently, 'Head for the jeep, Tascha.'

'But what about you?'

'I'll follow. Just do as I say.'

She had never heard that note in his voice before. Her wet feet squishing at every step, she hurried towards the jeep and all the safety that it represented, and heard Seth addressing the bear with far more authority than she had been able to muster. His movements were smooth and unhurried; he did not look at all afraid. He also was backing slowly towards the road, always keeping his body between her and the bear, talking in a steady monotone that she did not attempt to decipher.

The retreat to the jeep seemed to take for ever. But finally Tascha was scrabbling up the bank, grabbing at boulders with her fingers, digging for footholds with her toes. She opened the passenger door of the jeep and saw that Seth had left the driver's side open. Then she looked back over her shoulder.

The bear was still standing at the edge of the bog, and even as she watched it began nosing at the willows as if all along that had been its only interest. Seth was perhaps sixty feet from the road. She waited, every muscle tense, for to her over-stimulated imagination it still seemed as though the bear could gallop across the tundra and reach Seth before Seth could reach the jeep. But then the bear began to paw the ground at the base of a willow shrub, as if it had found a succulent shoot to eat; from a distance, its antics looked comical, particularly when some clods of earth flew up from its front paws. Tascha, however, did not laugh.

Seth climbed the bank with more *élan* than she had. Tascha was standing facing him, her hands at her sides, her face still deadly pale, her eyes huge. She was fully expecting him to be angry with her for venturing out alone, and braced herself for a tirade. Instead, he looked back over his shoulder at the bear, now hind-end-on as it snuffled at the willows, then folded his arms around her, pulled her close to his body and held her there.

She was safe! Her body began to shudder in violent reaction. She clutched at his shirt, burrowed her face into his shoulder and muttered in deep shame, 'I—I'm sorry. But I was so scared, I've never been so scared in my whole life, not even with the wolves. I looked up and there it was, and it kept looking at me and then it'd step nearer, and if you hadn't told me not to I would have run, I know I would.'

'I'm glad you didn't. He wasn't really that interested in you, but if you'd run he might have taken it into his head to chase you.'

'How do you know it's a he?' she stammered.

'It's the young male who's been hanging around all summer...you did well, Tascha. You kept your cool beautifully.'

'I kept thinking about everything you'd s-said,' she answered between chattering teeth, and added with a giggle that hovered on the edge of hysteria, 'I even sang *Edelweiss* to him.'

Seth gave her a squeeze. 'That must have been when he started going the opposite way. It's OK, you did everything right. It's OK...'

He was rocking her back and forth as if she were a child in need of comfort, and it was this as much as anything that made Tascha struggle to control her trembling limbs. Eventually she raised her head. 'I'm all right now,' she said, and tried to move away from him.

'Will you marry me, Tascha?' Seth said.

She blinked. 'Seth, don't play games—not now.'

'I'm not. I mean every word I'm saying.' Unconsciously, his arms tightened around her. 'When I came over the hill and saw you down there in the marsh with the bear, I was more frightened than I've ever been in all my years in the north—because I wasn't frightened for myself, I was frightened for you. You were in danger. And had he charged you then, I wouldn't have reached you in time. That's when I knew I'd been a fool, that I'd been frightened of all the wrong things. I hadn't dared to admit to myself that I love you, because one day you might die and I'd be left like my father. But when I saw you in danger, my biggest fear was that I'd never be able to tell you I loved you, that I'd never be able to begin loving you. That would have been the tragedy, Tascha, the loss...never to have loved you at all.'

She was staring at him with dazed blue eyes, immobile in his arms. He smiled at her with immense tenderness. 'I love you, Tascha—will you marry me?'

She managed a smile. 'I'm not dreaming? I haven't died of fright and gone to heaven?'

Seth grinned. 'With muddy feet like that? They wouldn't let you in.'

'If you truly love me and want to marry me, that's as near to heaven as I can get.'

'I probably fell in love with you when you marched into the Scagway Tavern and swore at them all in French. Why else do you think I was so hell-bent on keeping you away from the lodge? It wasn't just Andrei. I think I knew even then that I was vulnerable to you in a way I'd never been with anyone else. Those big blue eyes of yours seemed to see right through all my defences... oh yes, I was running scared! Tascha, you haven't answered my question.'

'Of course I'll marry you, Seth,' she said, her eyes shining. 'And I love you more than I can say.'

'Thank God!' He kissed her thoroughly, then added, 'On the next trip to Whitehorse?'

'Yes.' Tascha gave a laugh of pure happiness. 'My father can give me away.'

'I've just come from there.' Seth looked rueful. 'I somehow don't think he'll be surprised.'

'So that's where you went...'

'I had to. I've never known what jealousy meant until I saw you with Clyde—it tore me apart. I could have fed Clyde to the eagles piece by piece. But what right did I have to feel that way? None whatsoever. So I went to see Andrei, who's the wisest person I've ever known, and told him the way I was feeling. I even told him you and I had made love.'

'Did he haul out the shotgun?'

'No. He seemed to think it was very natural we should have made love. And then we talked about my parents. He told me that yes, my parents loved each other, but it was an ingrown love, selfish and immature. He told

me that my father fell in love with his grief in the same
way he had been in love with my mother, so that the
grief became as all-absorbing as the love had been. True
love, said Andrei, is not like that. He also said I was a
very different man from my father... in all the years
we've known each other, Andrei has never talked so
frankly about my parents.'

'You probably weren't ready to listen.'

'Which he would have been wise enough to know.'

Tascha gave Seth a sympathetic smile. 'So then you
were driving home and saw me hobnobbing with a
grizzly.'

'And thought all this hard-earned wisdom had been
learned too late,' Seth finished grimly. 'Too late—what
horrible words they are!'

'But we aren't too late. We have a lifetime ahead of
us.'

He kissed her again, passionately and explicitly. 'I
want to make love to you again, Tascha,' he said huskily.
'That was the most beautiful experience of my life.'

'Of mine, too... but let's not make love here. The
bear might change his mind.'

'We're also in full view of the lodge windows,' Seth
replied. 'Can't risk upsetting Clyde. Or Jasmine.'

'Your cabin or my tent?'

'My cabin—in case it rains.' He ducked, laughing, as
Tascha swung her fist at him. 'With any luck, everyone
at the lodge will be in bed,' he added, suddenly sobering.
'I don't want to wait, Tascha—I love you too much.'

But when they drove through the gate to the lodge,
there were fourteen people waiting for them, Martin and
Mae in the forefront, all the guests behind. 'Jasmine
spotted you with the bear!' Martin exclaimed. 'But, by
the time I'd got the bus started to go to your rescue,
Seth had arrived in the jeep.'

'I thought you were a goner,' Jasmine shuddered. 'You sure looked scared.'

'You mean, everyone saw me singing?' Tascha groaned. 'At least you couldn't hear me.'

'Then Seth came and saved you,' Jasmine sighed. 'It was very romantic. We were all taking turns watching in the telescopes.'

Seth said drily, 'I should think that must have been the most public proposal in the entire history of the Northwest Territories.'

'Proposal?' Jasmine and Mae squeaked in unison.

'She said yes, too,' Seth added, as an afterthought.

Jasmine threw her arms around Tascha. 'I wish it could have been me, but if it isn't, I'm glad it's you.'

'Took you long enough, Seth,' Mae said tartly.

'Isn't it a good thing you got the 'flu, though?' Seth responded, a gleam in his eye.

Mae bridled. 'Someone had to do something. The two of you were meant for each other.'

Clyde said a little over-heartily, 'Indeed you are.'

Tascha smiled. 'Thanks, Clyde.' Then everyone else crowded round to congratulate them and the party moved indoors, where Martin produced four bottles of extremely good wine in lieu of champagne. Mae, in her element, concocted a tray of hors-d'oeuvres which Jasmine passed around, and it was well after midnight by the time Tascha and Seth were left alone in the kitchen.

Mae had overindulged in the wine, had become very lachrymose as a result and had had to be guided to her cabin by Martin. As a consequence, the kitchen was littered with used wineglasses, dirty plates and crumpled serviettes. Tascha began to laugh. 'Mae's sure to have a hangover in the morning—so guess who'll be cleaning up the mess!'

'The bride-to-be,' Seth grinned. 'Treat me nicely and I might help you.'

'Bribery, eh?' said Tascha demurely. 'How will I treat you nicely, Seth?'

He caught her by the hand. 'Come to my cabin and I'll show you.'

Breakfast was an hour late the next morning.

"GIVE YOUR HEART TO HARLEQUIN" SWEEPSTAKES

OFFICIAL RULES

NO PURCHASE NECESSARY TO ENTER OR RECEIVE A PRIZE

1. To enter and join the Harlequin Reader Service, rub off the concealment device on all game tickets. This w
reveal the values for each Sweepstakes entry number and the number of free books you will receive. Accepti
the free books will automatically entitle you to also receive a free bonus gift. If you do not wish to take adva
tage of our introduction to the Harlequin Reader Service but wish to enter the Sweepstakes only, rub off
concealment device on tickets #1-3 only. To enter, return your entire sheet of tickets. Incomplete and/or
accurate entries are not eligible for that section or sections of prizes. Not responsible for mutilated or unrea
able entries or inadvertent printing errors. Mechanically reproduced entries are null and void.

2. Either way, your Sweepstakes numbers will be compared against the list of winning numbers generated at ra
dom by computer. In the event that all prizes are not claimed, random drawings will be held from all entr
received from all presentations to award all unclaimed prizes. All cash prizes are payable in U.S. funds. This
in addition to any free, surprise or mystery gifts that might be offered. The following prizes are awarded in th
sweepstakes:

(1)	*Grand Prize	$1,000,000	Annuity
(1)	First Prize	$35,000	
(1)	Second Prize	$10,000	
(3)	Third Prize	$5,000	
(10)	Fourth Prize	$1,000	
(25)	Fifth Prize	$500	
(5000)	Sixth Prize	$5	

*The Grand Prize is payable through a $1,000,000 annuity. Winner may elect to receive $25,000 a year for
years, totaling up to $1,000,000 without interest, or $350,000 in one cash payment. Winners selected will
ceive the prizes offered in the Sweepstakes promotion they receive.
Entrants may cancel the Reader Service at any time without cost or obligation to buy (see details in cen
insert card).

3. Versions of this Sweepstakes with different graphics may appear in other mailings or at retail outlets by Tors
Corp. and its affiliates. This promotion is being conducted under the supervision of Marden-Kane, Inc., an
dependent judging organization. By entering the Sweepstakes, each entrant accepts and agrees to be bou
by these rules and the decisions of the judges, which shall be final and binding. Odds of winning are depende
upon the total number of entries received. Taxes, if any, are the sole responsibility of the winners. Prizes a
nontransferable. All entries must be received by March 31, 1990. The drawing will take place on April 30, 199
at the offices of Marden-Kane, Inc., Lake Success, N.Y.

4. This offer is open to residents of the U.S., Great Britain and Canada, 18 years or older, except employees
Torstar Corp., its affiliates, and subsidiaries, Marden-Kane, Inc. and all other agencies and persons connect
with conducting this Sweepstakes. All federal, state and local laws apply. Void wherever prohibited or
stricted by law.

5. Winners will be notified by mail and may be required to execute an affidavit of eligibility and release that mu
be returned within 14 days after notification. Canadian winners will be required to answer a skill-testing que
tion. Winners consent to the use of their name, photograph and/or likeness for advertising and publicity
conjunction with this and similar promotions without additional compensation. One prize per family or househol

6. For a list of our most current major prizewinners, send a stamped, self-addressed envelope to: WINNERS LIS
c/o MARDEN-KANE, INC., P.O. BOX 701, SAYREVILLE, N.J. 08872

LTY-H

Harlequin American Romance

Romances that go one step farther...
American Romance

Realistic stories involving people you can relate to and
care about.

Compelling relationships between the mature men and
women of today's world.

Romances that capture the core of genuine emotions
between a man and a woman.

Join us each month for four new titles wherever paperback
books are sold.
Enter the world of American Romance.
